"Opposites attrac

Charlie grinned down a̲̲ ̲ ̲ ̲ ̲ ̲ ̲ ̲ ̲ ̲ ̲ ̲ ̲ ̲ ̲ ̲ ̲ ̲ on the best authority. I watch Oprah."

As always, Cassie's heart thudded in her chest when she looked up into his laughing gray eyes. "Oh, really? You're probably the only man around the agency who has time to watch Oprah. And what if we're wrong about Fran and Joe?"

"Well, then, I suppose we'll have our first date."

"This isn't a date," she reminded him, willing herself to ignore the heat spreading through her body.

"You're right," he said, a glint entering his eyes. "It's a mission. A cause. We're helping out two friends, buddies in arms. It's noble, self-sacrificing. It's got your name written all over it, Armstrong."

"Grow up, Whitman." She grabbed her purse. "Are you going to tease me all night?"

"Probably. You got a problem with that?"

"No," she said, thinking she'd have even bigger problems if Charlie Whitman ever got serious.

Susan Worth is the mother of two small children who writes "for personal sanity," or, as her husband puts it, "escape into fiction." For *Commitments*, her first Temptation, she escaped into her past—a ten-year career in the exciting world of New York advertising, where, as she says, truth is often stranger than fiction. Presently living in Virginia and employed as an insurance analyst in the medical field, Susan is working on her second book and her future career as a novelist.

COMMITMENTS
Susan Worth

Harlequin Books

TORONTO • NEW YORK • LONDON
AMSTERDAM • PARIS • SYDNEY • HAMBURG
STOCKHOLM • ATHENS • TOKYO • MILAN
MADRID • WARSAW • BUDAPEST • AUCKLAND

ISBN 0-373-25680-9

COMMITMENTS

Copyright © 1996 by Susan Gunter

1

THOUGH HE'D WORKED at Woodson & Meyers Advertising, Inc. a mere two days, Charlie Whitman could have scripted the agency's annual client Christmas dance. It could have been a set for a commercial, the ballroom of the Manhattan hotel looked appropriately elegant, the guests suitably chic and well connected, more like television versions of themselves than themselves. The liquor and rich food flowed freely, particularly the liquor, and Charlie knew that by evening's end, several elegant swells would be carted off dead drunk and several affairs started. This was not sheer cynicism on Charlie's part; it was advertising. Advertising, for all its unpredictability, was very predictable. The only problem was that Charlie Whitman, a true restless spirit, preferred the new and different over the predictable every time.

And then he saw her on the far side of the room. She had thick shoulder-length hair the color of taffy and blue, blue eyes, so blue a man could lose himself in them. In this overdressed, overbejeweled crowd, she stood out like a beacon in her simple red dress. She also wore the slightly frazzled air of a person in charge, wielding a clipboard while those around her hoisted champagne flutes.

Heading up the agency Christmas party, Charlie thought with a shake of his head; a sucker's job if ever there was one.

Unaware that she was being watched, the lady in red was engaged in earnest conversation with the penguin-coated figure of the maître d'. She pointed at a melting ice sculpture of what was once undoubtedly a swan but now resembled a mutant duck, and judging from the hectic spots of color that stained her cheeks, this was clearly not the lady's night with fowl.

Now here, Charlie thought, was something new and different. She wasn't the most chic woman in the room. Not even the most beautiful. Advertising attracted the pert and the perfect, the WASP and the WASP wanna-bes with disgusting regularity. But something about this woman drew him like a magnet. Instant attraction, he decided in one breath; instant trouble, he added in the next. He usually avoided the earnest type like the plague—they made him nervous—but he couldn't seem to stop looking at the lady in red, either. She made him smile.

New to the agency, but not to the business, Charlie was acquainted, at least by reputation, with most of the agency people in the room. But he didn't know her. Yet.

He turned to his newest partner in crime. "So who's the Ivory girl?"

Happily munching on a chicken wing, Joe Mancini paused long enough to mutter, "Huh?"

A short, stocky man with an oversize mustache that hid his face, Joe Mancini was a genius with visuals, a wizard of pictures, but like most art directors, he treated the English language as if it was some obscure means of communication. Fortunately for both their careers, words fell in Charlie the copywriter's domain. "The woman in red. Over there. What's her story?"

Peering over his chicken wing, Joe managed a record-breaking five consecutive words. "Oh. Cassie Armstrong. Account supervisor." Then, with a look of relief, he returned to his food.

Charlie sighed; he'd been hoping for more than name, rank and serial number. Working in an agency was like working in a goldfish bowl; everybody made it their business to know everybody else's business. But then Joe was so shy he was like a seventh-grade boy in a man's body. "I want details, man, details. What's she like? Who's she sleeping with? What are her innermost secrets? Her innermost fears?"

A tiny quiche dangling from his huge paw, Joe was clearly daunted. Nonetheless he managed to reply, "She's an account supervisor. I think she's got a boyfriend. She's . . . nice."

Ignoring the boyfriend part, Charlie concentrated on this second nugget of information. An account person who was nice? Impossible. Like most creatives, he held to the belief that account managers had been put on earth to drive the creative department crazy, their sole mission being to take the creative out of the creative product and then to take credit for somebody else's ideas. Still, Charlie thought, this Cassie Armstrong looked nice, at least from afar. He had only one further question for his friend. "What account's she on?"

"Ours. Majik Toys."

Charlie smiled. He was starting to like his job better already.

No one would ever accuse Charlie Whitman of altruism, but impulsiveness was another story. Without stopping to think about what he was doing or what he planned to do when he got there, he started across the room.

"Hey, where you goin'?" Joe called after him.

"To rescue a damsel in distress," he called cheerfully over his shoulder.

To which Joe, being Joe, muttered, "Huh?"

CLOSING IN on the battling duo, Charlie overhead their heated debate.

"Lady, like I keep telling you, I don't do ice sculptures. I'm the maître d', okay? I do food, I do beverage, but I don't do ice sculptures. Union rules."

And then Cassie Armstrong's more frantic tone. "But it's melting all over my appetizer table. I'm not asking you to fix it, just take it away please, before it drowns my endive salad."

"Lady, I'm not interested in your endive salad."

What they had here was a true Mexican standoff, New York style. Sensing diplomatic relations were strained to the breaking point, Charlie stepped into the fray. "Perhaps I can suggest a solution here?"

Two pairs of eyes, one slightly frantic, the other decidedly belligerent, swung toward him. The belligerent one took the lead.

"Who the hell are you?"

Now that, Cassandra Armstrong thought, was an excellent question. Perhaps the only intelligent thing uttered by the hotel employee throughout this entire exchange. She thought she knew most of the people in the room, but she most certainly did not know this tall stranger with the curly brown hair and lively gray eyes.

She would have remembered those eyes. They had an unforgettable air of mischief about them.

Though she would have welcomed just about any solution right about now, being a cautious person by nature, she hesitated. "Are you a client?" she asked politely, hoping, praying he was not.

"Bite your tongue, woman." He looked so insulted at the mere suggestion Cassie might have laughed had the situation been less serious. "No, think of me as a neutral third party... like Switzerland."

As Cassie and the maître d' exchanged wide-eyed stares, Charlie pressed home his advantage. "Look, Tom," he said pleasantly, reading the brass name tag on the man's penguin jacket. "Your union principles aside—and I'm a union man myself so I understand your loyalties—just what will it take to make this melting monstrosity disappear?"

A faint pause ensued as union loyalty warred with enlightened self-interest in the man's eyes. And unlike Cassie, Charlie was not in the least surprised when self-interest won the war. "Fifty bucks," he muttered.

"Done." Extracting his wallet, Charlie peeled off a handful of bills. Money talks, the swan walks.

And as the dying swan moved off in the direction of the kitchen, it occurred to Cassie that this stranger had accomplished in thirty seconds what she had been trying to do for most of the night.

Turning to the woman beside him, Charlie grinned at the stunned disbelief in her eyes. "You owe me fifty bucks. Not to mention your undying gratitude. Fortunately for you, I'll let you work it off with a dance."

"Bribery," Cassie mused. "Why didn't I think of that?"

He laughed. "Because you're a nice person. You have principles. That's two major character flaws."

"Do I know you?"

"No . . . but you will. Now about that dance . . ."

For the first time, Cassie looked at the man next to her—really looked at him—and was tempted by what she saw. With that tall, lanky body and curly brown hair, he was boyishly appealing rather than classically handsome. His nose just missed aquiline. His body didn't shout personal trainer. But that devastating grin and the lively intelligence in those gray eyes held a unique appeal of their own. It was his eyes that compelled her most of all. They promised life and laughter, and she could use some of both. Still, thinking of all she had to do, she resisted temptation. "Oh, no. I'm sorry. Thank you, but I can't. I have to check on the entrées and then there's the . . ."

All the while smiling at her, he ignored her words. Carelessly tossing her clipboard onto the table, he snagged her hand in his. And as the band broke into a somewhat syrupy rendition of "You Made Me Love You," Cassie instinctively matched her steps to his.

Not entirely sure how she'd gotten onto the dance floor, she tried again. "I really shouldn't be doing this."

"Relax." He drew her close. She felt good in his arms, tall but not too tall, thin but not too thin. Unlike the anorexic beauties waltzing around them, this woman seemed healthy, natural. "You're not working now. I told you, I'm not a client."

Breathlessly, Cassie pulled away. He was holding her far too close. "Then you're with the agency?" But she knew all the agency people in the room.

"I'm ordering you to relax," Charlie commanded, drawing her near again. "This is for your own good. Think of it as therapy."

She stopped resisting long enough to glance at his tux and frown. "You aren't wearing a name tag. Everybody's supposed to be wearing a name tag."

"I was never very good at rules," he informed her smoothly. "And I resist all labels."

"I see," she murmured, not at all sure that she did.

Charlie laughed and twirled her around. "And I can see you're a literal person, so I want you to repeat after me—this is advertising, it is not, I repeat not, a serious business."

"Advertising is not a—" She stopped, glanced into those lively gray eyes. "It isn't?"

"Of course not. This is the industry that brought you the Tidy Bowl man, Mr. Whipple and raisins that break into spontaneous Marvin Gaye hits. Trust me, this ain't brain surgery."

For the first time in hours, Cassie burst out laughing. Gratified, Charlie grinned at her. "I knew I could make you do that sooner or later." Her eyes were not any ordinary shade of blue, but a deep, rich, cornflower hue that somehow made him think of English gardens and old-fashioned high teas. "So how'd you get conned into heading up this little shindig, anyway?"

"That's a good question." A very good question. The same way, she supposed, she got conned into so many commitments. For a woman almost thirty years old, a woman who held a Master's degree in English and was certified to teach at the secondary level, it galled her to admit that after six years in the agency game she still hadn't caught on to its rules. Or maybe the problem was, nobody else seemed to be playing by any rules. "They were very persuasive," she added with a sigh.

"They usually are. That's how agency types get to be agency types."

"I know that." She bit her lip. "Now." Which reminded her . . . "I really should see about those entrées."

She tried to pull away, but he wouldn't let her go.

"No, I can't do this."

"Come on, just a little more."

Those gray eyes twinkled even as they persuaded, and Cassie felt her resistance weaken. "Well, I . . ."

He tightened his hold on her. "Relax. Look around this place. Judging from the crowd by the bar, you could serve Alpo with a cherry for dinner and they'd pronounce it delightfully piquant."

Cassie had to laugh . . . and admit he was right. She glanced at the couple next to them, to see a fast-food franchisee elaborately dip the media director in a move that in no way matched the rhythm of the music. The atmosphere was definitely loosening up, and it was only the appetizer course. "I can't imagine—" she sighed "—why the agency doesn't insist on dates for these affairs."

"I think affairs is the operative word here." Charlie grinned as the fast-food maven barely recovered his hold on the media mogul, then celebrated his dancing prowess by caressing her sequined bottom. "We work hard and we play hard," he whispered close to her ear.

"They're married," Cassie told him in a low tone, then added in an entirely different voice, "Too bad not to each another."

"I take it you don't approve?"

"Well, what's the point of being married?"

"I never saw it myself." Even as he said it, he drew her closer. "So what's a nice girl like you doing in a place like this?"

"That is a trite and tired line, whoever you are."

"This is a trite and tired business. So I repeat, what's a nice girl like you doing in a place like this?"

"That shows how much you know. I am sophisticated and urbane, just like everyone else in this room."

"Sorry." Smiling at her, he shook his head. "Not with those Ivory-girl looks and not with those eyes. You have very expressive eyes, you know. They give away everything you're thinking and feeling."

"They do not." Feeling challenged, she tried to match him stare for stare, but at his knowing grin, her gaze drifted away.

Charlie laughed. Nice, he thought. Joe was right. Cassie Armstrong was nice, very nice. Even her hair smelled nice, like honeysuckle. She made him think of spring mornings and innocent pleasures. Or maybe not-so-innocent pleasures. His grip tightened and his hands moved lower to mold her body more fully against his.

Her ice sculpture wasn't the only thing that was melting, Cassie thought, and she wasn't entirely sure she liked the sensation. She preferred being in control, at least until she knew what she was getting into. She was an analyzer, a planner, not the type to fall for strangers, not even very attractive ones with lively gray eyes. Wanting, needing the space, she deliberately drew back. "You know, you still haven't told me your name."

Charlie amended his earlier description—nice, but serious. "Do you always feel the need to label everything?"

"Always," she answered firmly, this time matching him stare for stare.

Tough, too, he thought, beneath that soft exterior. Wanting to tease her a little just to watch the reaction in those blue eyes, he answered, "I believe you, Cassie Armstrong, account supervisor on the Majik Toy account. A woman rumored around the agency to be nice, and to have a boyfriend."

He was not disappointed. Shock flooded her eyes. "Do I know you?" She answered her own question. "No, I know I don't know you. But then how do you know so much about me?"

He took pity on her. "A little bird told me. A very quiet little bird." He jerked his head toward Joe, who still occupied the far corner in blissful solitude.

"Aha." Recognition sprang into her expression. "You're Charlie Whitman, as in Charlie Whitman the new copywriter on the Majik Toy account, my account. I should have guessed right away."

He grinned. "Bingo. In the flesh."

Her eyes narrowed. "You're not going to give me any trouble, are you?" Ridiculous question to ask of a man who'd bribed a hotel employee, lied about holding a union card, refused to wear a name tag and had practically seduced her on the dance floor.

As if he'd read her mind, his eyes widened boyishly. "I'm sure I don't know what you mean."

"I'm sure you do. I have my own little bird." Except opinionated Fran wasn't so quiet. "And according to my unimpeachable source, you are known as being good, very good, but you insist upon having your own way, are chronically late with assignments and don't take direction very well. In short, an account person's nightmare." She paused for breath. "How am I doing so far?"

"Fair," he conceded with a grin. "You see why I hate labels."

"Oh, there's more," Cassie continued, gathering breath and steam. "You are also known for your inability to commit. In fact, you've worked at five different agencies in fourteen years, earning you the nickname around the industry of Charlie I'll-Try-Anything-for-a-Year Whitman." She might have also added that at age thirty-six, he had never been married, not even engaged, but she didn't want to get too personal. "Ring any bells, Charlie Whitman?"

"Not a one. And I'll prove it to you. You want commitment? Okay, marry me and have my babies."

He was so outrageous, Cassie had to laugh.

He pretended chagrin. "You don't believe me?"

"Sorry, I may be nice, but I wasn't born yesterday. You just don't strike me as the marrying kind."

"Okay, then," he conceded readily. "How about a cheap, sweaty and disgustingly meaningless affair where we'll wake up mortified in the morning and have to avoid each other around the agency for weeks?"

"You sound like the voice of experience."

He shook his head. "Pure conjecture. So what do you think?"

"You make it sound so tempting, but I just don't think so. As you pointed out I'm just not the affair type."

He sighed deeply. "You are a hard woman to please. Okay, but I warn you, this is my final pitch. How about a nightcap after the dance?"

Expecting the outrageous, she started to laugh, but something in his expression stopped her. Curious, she tilted her head to stare at him. "Are you asking me out?"

Now it was his turn to laugh. "Well, yes, that was the general idea. So what do you say?"

She was too surprised to know what to say. She wouldn't have thought she was Charlie Whitman's type. She wouldn't have thought he was hers. And yet she realized she was tempted, very tempted.

He cut into her thoughts. "I'm asking for a nightcap here, Armstrong, not a lifetime commitment. Your answer, please."

"I, ah, I'm seeing someone already."

"Aha!" Charlie pounced. "So the boyfriend rumor was true."

Though she could have told him then and there that Jeff Paulson was not exactly her boyfriend, she didn't. She liked to take things slow, liked to look before she leaped, and besides, she never got the chance as Charlie peppered her with questions.

"You're not married, Armstrong, are you?"

"Of course not."

"Engaged?"

"No."

"Pinned? Exchanged friendship rings? And I'm sorry, if he gave you a ring out of his Cracker Jack box when you were both four, that doesn't count."

She bit her lip to keep from laughing. "I don't like to date two people at the same time."

Charlie arched a brow. "Let me see if I get this straight. You live in Sodom and Gomorrah on the Hudson, you work in an industry where every other person is sleeping with every other person and where adultery is considered a sport, not a vice. But you don't date two people at the same time. Is that the general gist of things?"

"In a nutshell," she told him. "Besides, I don't usually go out with people I work with."

"Of course not." He shook his head in wonderment. "You really are a woman of principle, Cassie Armstrong. That's going to get you into trouble one of these days."

She suspected she was already there. Glancing around the dance floor, she found it completely empty save for Charlie and herself. Even the band had disappeared. She hadn't heard the song end, or noticed dinner being served. "Oh, my goodness!" She pulled out of his arms. "The entrées. I forgot all about them. I've got to go."

Reluctantly, he released her, smiling at her hurried pace toward the kitchen. A blur in red, he thought, shaking his head. "Hey, Armstrong," he called after her. "It ain't brain surgery."

But Cassie was already gone.

DESPITE ALL her worrying, or maybe because of it, the evening went off without a single hitch. Even the president of the agency stopped by to congratulate her on a job well done. Of course the man was three sheets to the wind at the time and probably wouldn't remember a word of it in the morning. Still, Cassie experienced the pleasant glow of a job well done.

She saw Charlie Whitman only twice more during the evening. The first time she sought him out.

"Oh, here you are!" She caught him by the bar as he was heading to his table. "I've been looking all over for you."

Those gray eyes sparkled. "And here I thought you didn't care."

She reached up to affix a name tag to his tuxedo jacket. "Wear it," she ordered, "and don't even think about taking it off."

"Yes, darling," he agreed dutifully, spanning her waist with his hands.

He laughed when Cassie immediately drew back a discreet pace. "Relax, Armstrong. Given the alcohol-to-hemoglobin content in this room, you could take off your clothes and streak naked through the place and nobody'd notice." A spark of mischief flashed in his eyes. "Say, you wouldn't care to—"

"Stop teasing me. I'm nervous enough already, without you teasing me."

"I will be good," he promised.

She only wished she believed him as she drew in a deep breath. "Okay, now you're seated with Vince Bertolli, the president of Majik Toys. Although what possessed me to put you there I'll never know. Of course, I didn't know you then." The thought of Charlie Whitman with the gruff, self-made captain of Majik Industries made the nervous quivers in Cassie's stomach metamorphose into giant butterflies. She gave him a stern look. "Behave yourself."

He smiled into her worried face. "I'll be a model of deportment, a veritable font of wit and charm. Scout's honor."

"You were a Boy Scout?" It was enough to destroy one's faith in the future of scouting in America forever.

"Hell, no. I suppose I'll just have to be myself."

That was exactly what Cassie feared most, Charlie Whitman being himself. Seated at the head table, she tried to concentrate on her chicken *cordon bleu* and the conversation around her, but found herself casting anxious and frequent glances toward Charlie's table. She needn't have worried. Rather than appearing offended, the toy magnate seemed bowled over by Woodson & Meyers's newest copywriter. She watched in amazement as her usually dour, grim-faced client threw back his head and roared at one of Charlie's remarks. *He never laughed like that for me*, Cassie thought with a stab of admiration, heavily laced with envy. Not that she ventured many witty remarks around the man. She was too terrified of his caustic, cutting, Brooklynese style to venture much of anything. Charlie Whitman didn't seem to be afraid of anybody or anything, and she envied his casual confidence. Or maybe the secret to his success was that he simply didn't care. Time would tell.

IN THEIR FINAL encounter of the evening, it was Charlie who sought Cassie out. "Congratulations," he said with a grin, his voice echoing in the nearly empty ballroom. Only the hotel cleaning crew and a handful of party-hardy stragglers remained. "You survived trial by advertising-client party. And I think only two people threw up. An unqualified success. So how do you feel, champ?"

Cassie laughed tiredly. "Like I've died, only somebody forgot to tell me, if you want to know the truth.

If anyone so much as mentions the agency Christmas party next year, promise me you'll shoot me first and put me out of my misery." She was so tired she could barely manage her coat and gratefully accepted Charlie's assistance when he stepped forward to help her with the sleeve. She drew back, pulling the lapels together and fixing her muffler. "So how'd you like your new client?"

"Who, old Vince?" Cassie arched a brow at that, and Charlie shrugged. "Not bad for a guy who's a dead ringer for a Mafia don. No ethnic slur intended, but I could just imagine old Vince making someone an offer they can't refuse."

Charlie Whitman was a perceptive man. "And it's usually someone in his ad agency," she said. "He could rival you in the commitment department, Charlie Whitman. Vince has fired three agencies in the last five years. I'm afraid we have our work cut out for us. And speaking of which—" she worried her bottom lip "—did you get my memo about the four alternative print ad concepts that are due in two weeks?"

"Probably." He sighed, watching the lines of tension return to her face. "Not to mention the strategy selection outline, the demographic profile for all twelve product lines and next year's advertising plans." Past their uninspiring titles, he hadn't glanced at a one, though he kept that fact to himself. "I've only been here two days, Armstrong, and already you've got me buried alive in paper. You are a busy little bee."

"We work hard and we play hard," she quoted him.

Impulsively, he reached forward to tweak her nose, laughing when she shied away. "Work is one thing, Cassie Armstrong, but you worry too much."

She started to defend herself, then stopped and shrugged. "You're right," she conceded with a sigh. "And I'm too tired to worry anymore tonight. Tomorrow is another day."

She did look tired. Exhausted was more like it. Pale smudges of violet marred those cornflower blue eyes. For some reason he couldn't quite fathom, he wanted to fix it, make it better. It was a most un-Charlie-like reaction. As he escorted her through the lobby and out into the cold, clear December night, he heard himself ask, "So, how about a lift home?"

But she was already shaking her head. "Thank you, and I'm flattered, but—"

"This isn't a pass, Armstrong. It's a ride home."

"Oh. Well, in that case . . ." The suggestion seemed harmless enough, and she was tired. She glanced at that curly brown hair, those lively gray eyes. "Where's your car?"

"Funny, that's just what I was about to ask you."

She turned to stare at him. "Charlie Whitman, are you trying to tell me . . ." As tired as she was, Cassie burst out laughing. "You are outrageous, Charlie Whitman." She caught his grin. "But then, I suppose you know that already."

A stray breeze ruffled her thick hair. "You've only got thirty seconds to make an impression. Better make it memorable."

Cassie laughed. "Well, it certainly has been that."

"Perhaps," he suggested delicately, "a compromise is in order here. We could share a cab. Dutch treat, of course." He slanted her a grin. "I wouldn't want to violate any of those strongly held principles of yours."

She forced down a smile, liking this man a lot, probably too much for her own good. "Perhaps," she agreed slowly. "I live uptown, Upper East Side."

"Uh-oh," Charlie groaned. "No compromise here." His eyes strayed over her good Republican cloth coat. "Although I should have guessed you were the uptown type." He regarded her loftily. "I'm a Soho man myself. Before gentrification, of course."

"Oh, of course." Smiling slightly, she noted he was coatless in December. "Very eclectic neighborhood. No rules."

"To each his own," Charlie told her with a grin.

"*Vive la difference*," she added.

He flagged down an approaching cab, then held open the door with a small flourish. "Your carriage awaits, milady."

Entering the idling taxi, she held out her hand. "To a rewarding and productive working relationship, Charlie Whitman."

Instead of shaking her hand, he favored her with a mock salute. "Let the games begin, Cassie Armstrong." With one final grin, he shut the door.

2

TWO WEEKS after Christmas, trapped on the telephone
with Vince Bertolli, sheer politeness forced Cassie to
allow her client to drone on. He would make a good
Mafia don, she thought, recalling Charlie Whitman's
description of the man. He certainly gave enough orders.

Glancing at her watch, she grimaced; the conference
report still had to be written, the creative brief had to
be edited. But Majik Toys, with its twelve product lines,
was an important account at Woodson & Meyers, and
she was paid to be polite. To be polite and to produce
good advertising. With Vince, the two often seemed
mutually exclusive. He might be a brilliant toy magnate, but the man had lousy creative instincts. "Of
course, of course," she assured him. "Of course, we'll
have the print concepts written by Friday. Yes, and
you'll get four alternatives...."

As she hung up the phone, she prayed she was right.
Grabbing her clipboard, she headed purposefully toward Charlie Whitman's office.

She hadn't seen him since the Christmas dance. She'd
been too busy. It seemed she wasn't the only one.

It wasn't just that his office was a chaotic mess—although there was that. Cassie's organized soul rebelled
at the littered confusion. Her eyes narrowed at the sight
of her hard-worked documents carelessly tossed about

and clearly unread. But what really stunned her, what stopped her dead in her tracks, was that instead of finding the agency's newest copywriter diligently at work on her account, she found a significant number of the agency's highly priced creative talents lounging about his office. They were swapping gossip about who was sleeping with whom while desultorily shooting wads of crumpled paper into a new addition to the room—a basketball hoop. And even as she stood there she overheard Charlie say to his band of Merry Men, "Hey, guys, did you hear the one about . . ."

Two weeks, Cassie thought, he'd only been here two weeks. Think of what this man could do in a month. A year. The possibilities boggled the mind.

Glancing up, Charlie spotted her, and just like the first time he'd met her, she made him smile. Clutching her clipboard like a talisman, she wore a buttercup yellow silk shirt and a dismayed expression. No poker player here. He assumed, correctly, that Cassie Armstrong did not approve of the way he'd livened things up around Woodson, et al. But man did not live by advertising alone. Now, to convince her of that.

"Uh-oh," Charlie teased. "Management type approaching at twelve o'clock. Man your battle stations. I repeat, man your battle stations."

"That isn't a management type," a mechanical artist drawled fondly. "That's Cassie."

"Yeah," another ventured. "She's nice."

Cassie zeroed in on the man behind the desk. "Thanks a lot, Whitman. You are a bad influence."

Grinning, he pretended to be hurt. "Who? Me? I've been telling these guys all afternoon that advertising is a serious business. They just won't listen."

Shaking her head, she waited until they were alone. "Well, Charlie, I was wondering how you were getting along." Her glance flicked to the basketball hoop. "I can see I needn't have worried."

Hands behind his head, displaying his Life Is Not A Dress Rehearsal T-shirt, he surveyed her with a grin. "You worry too much, Armstrong. I told you that. But I am touched you thought of me. Dare I hope this is a social call? Or better yet—" his grin turned sly "—is our affair still on?"

"Not exactly."

Charlie sighed. "I was afraid of that. But take a load off, Armstrong. Have a seat. You look like a woman who could use one."

"What I could use, Charlie Whitman, is four alternative print ads for Majik Toys. More specifically, the four alternative print ad concepts that were due to me today. The same print ads we have to present to the client on Friday."

She looked so serious he couldn't resist the urge to tease her. "My, my, has it been ten days already?"

"Yes, well…" Once again her gaze went to the hoop. "Time flies when you're having fun."

Not in the least abashed, he grinned. "I knew you'd understand, Armstrong. But hey, you can use it any time you want. Here, take a shot." He whistled admiringly when she effortlessly caught the balled-up paper he tossed to her. "Nice hands. You can be on my team anytime."

"Thank you. And you're changing the subject."

"Which was?"

"The print ads, Charlie. How are you coming on them?"

"Oh, just dotting the *i*'s and crossing the *t*'s." He sank a basket with practiced ease. "I don't like to pass out inferior work."

Her eyes narrowed. "In other words you haven't started them yet. " And then she leaned on the desk for support. "Charlie—"

He laughed again, this time in exasperation. "Armstrong, I order you to stop worrying. Now you said it yourself, those print ads aren't even due until Friday. This is Monday. Ergo—"

"Ergo nothing, Charlie Whitman. The client presentation is Friday. But I have to prepare what I'm going to say first, which is why—"

"You prepare what you're going to say?"

She stopped. "Well, yes, of course. Don't you?"

The thought had never crossed his mind. "I'm not a big believer in overrehearsing. I'm more a seat-of-the-pants kind of guy."

Now that, she had no trouble buying. "Charlie Whitman, I know you may find this hard to believe, but we're running a business around here. Now, I'm trying to be nice, but nobody plays around with my account...."

He stopped listening and watched instead. Though trying to look stern, she succeeded only in looking worried—worried and adorable. "Okay, okay," he heard himself say. "You win. No more Chinese water torture. I'll write them."

"...not when I'm in charge, so I suggest—"

"Armstrong, I said I'll write them."

She stopped, eyed him suspiciously. "When?"

"Now."

"Oh. You will?"

He had to laugh. "Yes, but only because you're too young and too pretty to work yourself into an ulcer."

"Gee, that wasn't too bad. And here I thought I'd have to drag out the whips and the chains."

Charlie's gray eyes sparkled. "Save that thought for after hours. Now give me—" He consulted his watch, then whistled through his teeth. "Do you know what time it is? I can't believe you have me staying late to finish an assignment that isn't even due yet. It's a good thing you're so pretty, Armstrong, because, you know, this goes against all my principles."

When opportunity presented itself, she couldn't resist the urge to pay him back, if only a little. "What was that, Charlie? What was that word I heard you use? Principles? And here I thought you didn't have any."

Those gray eyes focused on hers, dancing wickedly. "Are you teasing me, Armstrong? Because I warn you, I always get even."

At the look in those eyes, she believed him and backed down. "No, no, I'm sorry. It was a temporary aberration. I swear it'll never happen again."

"Too late." Before Cassie could react, before she could even guess what he was up to, he reached across the desk and grabbed the clipboard out of her hands.

She could only stare. "Charlie Whitman, what do you think you're doing? Give that back to me."

A glint in his eyes, he held it over his head. "You want it, come and get it."

"Charlie, this is not funny. I need that." Her lists dominated her life. "Now pretend you're a mature adult and hand it over."

"Sorry, mature-adult gibes don't work very well with me. I've been hearing them all my life. No, you're going to have to do better than that."

Disbelieving, she stared at him. "You're not suggesting that I chase you around the office, are you? That is totally juvenile."

He grinned. "You bet, but it's also a lot of fun."

Her eyes narrowed threateningly. "Charlie, if you don't give that to me, I'll—"

"You'll what, Armstrong? What are you going to do, call my mother?"

Almost despite herself, she started to smile. Better, Charlie thought. Much better.

"But you know," he told her, "you mature-adult types have always fascinated me. Just what is it you organized people write down on these lists of yours?" He glanced at her sheet. "Oh, now here's a salient item." He pretended to read from the list. "Remember to get dressed in the morning. What happens if you don't consult your list, Armstrong? Find yourself naked on Ninth? Bare-bottomed on Broadway?"

"It doesn't say that." But she was laughing.

On a roll, Charlie continued. "Oh, now here's another little gem. Remember to shower in the morning. Well, mankind certainly thanks you for that."

Laughing hard, Cassie lunged at him. "Give me that damned clipboard, Whitman."

She was fast, but he was faster. He leaped sideways, holding the clipboard over his head. "Oh, the principled Ms. Armstrong swearing in the office. Whatever is this world coming to?"

Cassie went for broke. Lunging again, this time she secured an edge of the clipboard. Victory was almost hers. She could taste it, feel it. Except Charlie swiped the clipboard from her tenuous grip, swinging it behind his back. In the process, Cassie lost her footing, falling against his chest.

"Hey, wait a minute, killer!" Still holding the clipboard behind his back with one hand, he gripped her about the waist with the other, steadying her.

He smiled into her eyes. "Nice try, Armstrong, but you lose."

"You think so, huh?" With an evil smile, she reached up and caught a hefty hunk of that curly hair . . . and pulled.

"Ow." Surprise widened his eyes. "That hurts. You fight dirty, lady."

"You betcha," she answered, totally unrepentant. "I don't have three brothers for nothing."

"Have mercy," he winced. "I'm an only child."

"Give me the clipboard, Charlie."

Even through the pain, he couldn't resist teasing her. "Okay, okay, I'm sorry I thought you were a cream puff."

"You thought I was a cream puff?" She pulled even harder.

"Ouch. No fair. You fight like a girl."

Breathing hard, she laughed at him. "I am a girl."

She felt like a girl, too. Rounded where she should be rounded, soft where she should be soft. Beneath his hand, the soft silk of her blouse felt sensuously smooth. Laughter fled as those gray eyes darkened. "So I noticed."

From the very first moment he'd laid eyes on her, he'd felt the pull of attraction between them. He felt it now, and Cassie did, too. He brought the hand holding the clipboard around to join the other behind her back. Cassie's grip loosened on his hair, and her hands drifted downward to rest on his shoulders.

Clipboard forgotten, their breathing quickened, although not from exertion. Time hung suspended as round blue eyes met lively gray ones. For one wildly crazy moment, she thought he was going to kiss her. For an even crazier moment, she thought she would let him.

A movement from the hallway broke the spell. Skittering backward, Cassie swallowed hard and fought for control. She refused to look at him, afraid of what she'd give away.

More than a little shaken, Charlie didn't notice. Kissing an account person in the office? That was a new one, even for him and his lifetime of outrageous stunts. Then again, he'd never before met an account person he wanted to kiss in the office. Cassie Armstrong was full of surprises, he decided, thinking about the hair pulling. Fun surprises for such a serious person. Wondering how she was taking all this, he glanced over, caught, with some delight, her blush, and of course felt compelled to comment upon it.

"You know, Armstrong, I don't think I've seen a woman blush since 1970. No, make that 1966."

"This is not a blush." Though of course it was. "This is rage."

"Funny." He grinned. "It looks just like a blush."

"No, I'm telling you it's rage. Now give me that clipboard before I'm forced to get really tough with you." She held out a hand, saw him hesitate. "Please."

"Well, if you're going to use the magic word . . ." He passed it over.

She reminded herself to keep it businesslike. "I also need those concepts, Charlie."

"You're not much fun today, Armstrong." He sighed. "But okay. Give me half an hour. Your office. Be there."

She cast him a skeptical look. "You're going to write four print ads in thirty minutes?"

On surer ground, Charlie grinned. "No, I'm going to write four award-winning print ads in half an hour."

"You're pretty sure of yourself, Whitman."

He cocked a brow. "One of us has to be."

Given the way Cassie Armstrong hurriedly left the room, he supposed he'd gotten the last word. Still, she actually had him staying late at the agency to complete an ad that wasn't even due yet. A first for Charlie Whitman. A draw, he decided. The contest had definitely been a draw.

PROMPTLY thirty minutes later, he rapped smartly on her office door. Cassie glanced up, and her eyes widened. "You're done? Already?"

"When you're good, you're good." His voice was smug, but not for long. Looking around, he stopped dead in his tracks. "You're so neat!" File folders marched smartly in their assigned compartments, pens gleamed from their holders, caps on. There was not so much as a paper clip out of place. "What do you do, Armstrong?" he asked, only half joking. "Rent this place out as an operating room after hours? Your desk is so empty, it looks like you quit."

"What's wrong with being organized?" And then she caught herself. "And just how is it, Charlie Whitman, that you manage to turn all virtues into vices?"

"It's a rare gift. Cultivated over a lifetime of breaking all the rules. But don't worry, Armstrong, you'll catch on. You show a lot of potential."

Even as she shook her head, she had to smile. "Can I see the copy?"

He handed over several pages. "Read it and weep."

Glancing down, she motioned him into a chair, but he chose to prowl the room restlessly. The famed ego wall caught his attention first. Every office in advertising had one, except maybe his own. But then he had a basketball net, his own personal statement. A Master's degree in English, he observed. No surprises there. She was certainly bright enough, not to mention a stickler for detail. A framed photo caught his eye, and he picked it up. The Armstrongs, *en famille*. Had to be. He picked Cassie out of the crowd, smiling at the sight of her. Five healthy suntanned children and the requisite mother and father smiled back at him. Even a family dog had snuck into the pose. They looked like the Brady Bunch. "So where you from, Armstrong?"

Answering absently, she gave him her standard reply. "New York."

Half turning, he arched a brow. "You're from New York? No way." And then he caught on. "Upstate, right? Small town? You go to church every Sunday. Your father is a banker and your mother—" his eyes narrowed thoughtfully "—heads up the PTA and in her spare time is a member of the gardening club."

Her eyes lifted from the page. "That shows how much you know, Charlie Whitman. My dad runs a hardware store and my mother has no free time. Not with five children."

He grinned. "Sorry, I stand corrected." He replaced the picture on the credenza, thinking she was just the type to keep family reminders around. Of his own, there was none. He turned to face her. "So where's my competition, Armstrong?"

Her eyes drifted upward. "What?"

"The boyfriend. Where's the requisite boyfriend-in-the-last-dying-rays-of-the-sunset shot?"

"I don't—" Changing her mind, she eyed him sternly. "Would you please sit down? You're distracting me."

"Now, that sounds promising," he drawled, but he compromised by lounging against the arm of a chair. "What are you doing, memorizing that thing?"

"No, I'm trying to concentrate. And if you'd be quiet . . ."

At long last, she looked up from the page. "It's good," she announced. "It's very good. It meets the strategic objective. . . . The language fits the target audience. . . . The appeal is—"

"Is *perfect* the adjective you're striving for here?"

She supposed it was. Her eyes found his. "And this took you thirty minutes?"

"Twenty. It took me ten to find a damned pencil."

"You're supposed to be using the computer."

"Rules, rules, rules."

Cassie sighed. Life was not fair. Here she worked, slaved, for this business and this man effortlessly churned out what was undoubtedly an award-winning copy and he couldn't even find a stupid pencil in his office. From across the desk, she regarded him.

Managing to look both boyishly innocent and all too appealing at the same time, he returned her gaze. "So how about a reward for all my hard work? Have dinner with me. After all, you owe me one."

Her heart beat a little faster. "You want me to reward you for doing what was your job in the first place?"

"Armstrong." He sighed. "You are such a stickler. We are really going to have to work on that. And that isn't an answer to my question."

It wasn't. She probably shouldn't, she thought, remembering that almost kiss. She sensed Charlie Whitman was out of her league in the romance department, and the truth was, she wasn't much of a risk taker. Yet she couldn't seem to say no, either. There was something irresistible about this man. Instead, she stalled. "I really have to work, and so do you. And speaking of details, Whitman, just where are the other three award winners?"

"Have dinner with me and I'll work on them." Seeing her hesitate, he pressed home his advantage. "We'll compromise. I'll bring in Chinese or pizza. That way you can make sure I work. And even you have to eat. Come on, you couldn't ask for a fairer deal than that."

She supposed she couldn't. She supposed she didn't try very hard to resist.

ACROSS A PIZZA BOX, a slice in one hand, she tried to edit a conference report, all the while aware of Charlie's bright eyes upon her, the blank sheet before him.

Fighting down a blush, she managed to speak. "Charlie Whitman, you haven't written a thing."

He hadn't. He'd been distracted by thoughts of kissing her. She looked so serious, so earnest, hunched over her desk that the impulse was overwhelming. He wondered how she'd react if he did. It wasn't a thing he usually worried about with women, but Cassie Armstrong was different. He regarded her lightly. "You obviously don't understand the creative process, Armstrong. The work, the sweat, the agony that gets poured into every word. Why, it's like giving birth."

"Sorry," Cassie told him. "But I'm not buying. Not from a man who wrote a concept in under half an hour."

"You're right," Charlie replied mildly. "That's not the truth. The truth is, I'm distracted. The truth is, I was thinking about kissing you."

Cassie almost choked on her pizza. This time she couldn't quite control the blush and didn't miss the grin on his face. She tried to eye him sternly. "Are you making fun of me again, Charlie Whitman?"

"No, actually, I think I like you."

He hadn't meant to say that exactly; it had just slipped out. He was spared making a face-saving retort when Cassie notched together her papers in a move reminiscent of librarians and schoolteachers everywhere. "Well, that's enough work for tonight," she announced, reaching for her coat.

He gathered his own empty pages.

As she switched off the light, she said, "I still need three more concepts, Charlie."

"Why? What's so magical about four concepts, anyway? No pun intended, of course. The one I already wrote says it all."

She sighed. "Because Vince Bertolli likes to choose."

Which was exactly the way the Majik Toy campaign looked, Charlie thought. No synergy, no uniformity between the pieces—no campaign. Like someone had picked copy, eenie, meenie, minie, moe. He shook his head. "Cassie, that isn't very smart, letting Vince be in charge like this. We should be setting the strategy, not the client."

"I know, Charlie. I know that. But ol' Vince, as you like to call him, is one tough customer. He likes to think he's smarter than all of us agency types put together. And he always likes to have the last word."

The only problem was, so did Charlie Whitman.

Over the next few days, Cassie begged, pleaded, cajoled and stormed, but to no avail. The three missing alternative concepts remained missing. She threatened him with everything including personal injury; Charlie just shrugged and promised it in the morning. But even Charlie Whitman eventually ran out of mornings. The presentation loomed the next day when Cassie cornered him in the hall.

"Where are they, Whitman? No more excuses."

"They're going to be good," he promised. "They're just not done yet."

"They'd better be wonderful. They'd better be better than wonderful."

"Stop worrying, Cassie. They're going to knock your socks off."

He didn't lie. They certainly did.

THEY'D AGREED to meet early in the lobby of the Majik Toy building. She was here, where was he? Pacing the lobby, she'd bitten her nails to the quick, a habit she'd broken herself of in the third grade, by the time she heard unconcerned whistling from the revolving doors and Charlie Whitman appeared. He was suitably attired, for once, in a grown-up suit and tie, even if the tie was psychedelic. But Charlie Whitman's attire was the least of her worries. She took one look at his face and she knew.

"Oh, my God," she gasped. "You didn't write them, did you?"

"Nope," he agreed blithely. "We don't need them."

Shocked disbelief quickly transformed itself into anger. "I am going to kill you." Mindful of their surroundings, she lowered her voice and spoke through gritted teeth. "Just wait until I get you alone, Charlie Whitman. I'm going to draw and quarter you. I'm going to rip you limb from limb."

"Ooh, promises, promises," he shot back with a grin, then pointed an unrepentant finger at her face. The red of her business suit paled in comparison to her flaming cheeks. "Now *that's* rage."

Smoldering, she skewered him with an angry look. It didn't seem to faze him any more than threats had. Striving for logic, she took three deep breaths and forced herself to calm down. "Okay, look, we'll just cancel the meeting. We'll reschedule for next week. We could tell him you're sick. We could tell him you broke your leg." She glared at him. "In fact, I'll even break it for you." Pivoting on her heels, she started to stalk toward the street when his hand shot out to stop her. Gently grasping her by the elbow, he escorted her to the elevator.

"Where are we going?" she demanded. "We're going the wrong way."

Smiling at her, he pressed the button for up. "Don't be obtuse, Armstrong. You've been bugging me about this presentation for weeks. We're going to sell our client some top-notch copy."

"No, we're not, Charlie Whitman. We're going back to the agency."

She struggled against his grip, but he refused to let go. "Do you want to make a scene?"

Aware that he was only too capable of it, aware of the crowded lobby, she contented herself by furiously tapping her foot and dismembering him with her eyes. But once the elevator doors slammed shut, leaving them alone, all bets were off. She rounded on him furiously. "You're the one who's being obtuse, Charlie Whitman. Don't you understand who you're dealing with here? Do you have any idea what Vince Bertolli is like? He's going to fire us. He's fired everybody. And even if you don't care about yourself, Charlie I'll-Try-Anything-for-a-Year Whitman, what about the rest of us? What about me? What about the whole damned agency? Do you know what this loss of billing will mean, Charlie?" She answered it for him. "Jobs, Charlie. Everybody's jobs. Are you getting the picture now?"

In the face of her dire predictions, he was maddeningly calm about the whole thing. "I fail to see how presenting a client with a perfect concept, which even you agreed meets all the objectives, is going to get anybody fired."

But she was already shaking her head. "You don't know Vince. I told you, he insists upon making a choice between concepts." But she saw the closed look on Charlie's face, knew she was wasting her time. "Three weeks," she fumed. "You've been here three weeks and already you're a damned expert. I knew you were trouble, Charlie Whitman. I knew you were trouble from the very first moment I laid eyes on you."

Surprising them both, he grabbed her by the shoulders and swung her around, hard. The shock tactic worked. Though she was still fuming, he'd gotten her attention. "Look, Armstrong, Vince Bertolli wouldn't know good creativity if it bit him in the rear end. That's our job. We're the advertising experts. Not him. And despite what you may have heard, an account manager's job is not to make the client happy. It is not to kiss ass and it is not to suck up. Too many account people make that mistake, and they usually end up out on the street, burned-out at forty. I don't want to see you make that mistake. Your job is to see that Majik Toys has the best possible advertising campaign, which my concept delivers. *Capische?*"

Some of the anger left her eyes.

She had never known Charlie Whitman to be serious, didn't know he was capable of it, but he was all business now. And deep down, she knew he was right, at least mostly right. Still, she didn't appreciate his high-handed methods. Only partly mollified, she stabbed him with a disgruntled look. "You could have at least told me what you were going to do."

He smiled at her. "And you would have let me?"

In answer, Cassie looked away.

"Trust me, Armstrong," he said gently. "I've been at this business a little longer than you have. I won't steer you wrong."

The elevator thudded to a stop at the thirtieth floor, and with it Cassie's heart. Reaching for her hand, he squeezed it tight. "No guts, no glory," he told her with a grin. Nodding, she stepped out.

The Majik Toy reception area was housed behind glass doors at the far end of the building. As they passed down a long corridor hung with museum-quality oils by the great masters, she was reminded of just how powerful a man Vince Bertolli was. Which was precisely the point of the exhibit. "Vince collects art," she explained to Charlie even as her feet dragged, "the same way he collects agency heads." Suddenly, she stopped dead in her tracks, her eyes imploring. "Please, Charlie, please. This is a mistake. I know Vince better than you do. Let's go back. Please."

He had to admit it, even he had second thoughts. The collection had unnerved him, too. Except, deep down, he knew he was right. If they didn't start running this business, instead of letting Vince run them, eventually, they'd go the way of all their agency predecessors. Hiding all doubts, he smiled confidently. "No way, Armstrong. I'm not letting you off the hook that easy. Now let's go kick a little butt."

VINCE BERTOLLI, Charlie quickly surmised, was the worst kind of advertising client. He had no imagination, but thought he did. Not many people would dare to tell ol' Vince he was wrong, though. Like many self-made men, ol' Vince was a force to be reckoned with. You might be able to take the boy out of Brooklyn, but you couldn't quite take Brooklyn out of the boy. Behind those thousand-dollar custom-made suits lurked the heart of a street thug, which he undoubtedly had once been. Street smarts and raw power emanated from the man, and like any good godfather type, Vince Bertolli had piercing black eyes that could rip a person to shreds in a single glance. How, Charlie wondered, did this guy ever end up selling toys, of all things? Their client began the presentation with a single word. "Shoot."

Charlie laughed. When Vince didn't laugh back, he shifted uneasily, though he smiled confidently toward Cassie. *Come on*, he silently cheered, as she began the presentation. *You can do it.*

Meeting Charlie's eye, she took a deep breath and started selling hard. Amazing what a motivator sheer terror could be. She was giving the presentation of her life.

Facts and figures right at her fingertips, she made a wonderful case for his concept, clearly spelling out how it met each and every objective. And she only looked at her clipboard once. The moment of truth came as she wrapped things up. "And so, for these reasons, we're recommending this strategy for the Suzy Suzette line."

Vince shrugged one shoulder. "It's good. I like it."

Cassie breathed a sigh of relief. It proved a trifle premature, for in the next breath, Vince demanded, "So where are the other three? "

Cassie faltered. "I, ah . . ."

"Where are they, Armstrong? You know I need to see four concepts before I make any decisions."

"Well, ah . . ."

"Cat got your tongue today, Armstrong? Come on, I don't have all day here. Give me the others and let's get on with it."

"Well, ah . . . There aren't any others." There, she had finally gotten it out. The hard part was over—she hoped.

"Stop playing games, lady." As if sensing weakness, he closed in for the kill. "You know how many agencies there are out there? How many agency types? One phone call to your boss, and I could have you out in the street so fast . . ."

Direct hit, Cassie thought, stomach churning. She'd never get another job. Not in this recession. She'd have to move home. No way unemployment would cover her rent. Her parents would have to support her until she could get a teaching job.

Charlie jumped into the fray. "You don't need any other concepts . . . Vince." He deliberately chose the familiar term, even more deliberately sought her eyes. "Isn't that right, Cassie?"

Come on, Cassie, Charlie's eyes challenged her. *Do it. Say it. Don't back down now.*

She met his gaze. *No guts, no glory.* Tilting her head, she looked Vince square in the eye. "There are no other concepts, Mr. Bertolli. Because you don't need any more. This concept meets all the objectives we laid out. And—" she took a deep breath "—as the advertising experts for Majik Toys, we're standing behind this one. Now if you don't want me on this account, go ahead and make that call, but I believe that Majik Toys needs a more forceful advertising statement and I think . . . no, I *know* this concept is going to sell you a lot of toys."

Silence. The room was so quiet, Cassie swore she heard each and every agonizing beat of her own heart.

"Oh, hell," Vince said at last. "It's pretty good. Go with it."

Cassie almost dropped dead in relief.

Vince rose from his chair, then paused to cast a considering look in Charlie's direction. "This your idea, young man?"

"No, sir," Charlie answered. "As soon as Cassie read my ad she said, nope, that's it, this is the one. You can stop now."

Vince's eyes swung to Cassie. "Nice going, Armstrong. I had you figured for a soft touch, but I gotta admit it, I liked your moxie today. Nice hustle, kid. Keep up the good work."

She stared at him in disbelief. She'd worked so hard to win Vince's approval and the one time, the only time, she'd disobeyed him, he liked her style. She'd never figure out this business.

Charlie's bright gray eyes smiled into hers. "You did it, Armstrong. You really did it. I have to admit you had me worried there for a minute, but then you pulled it out. We're going to make a hardened advertising type out of you yet. Stick with me, kid."

She was feeling too weak at the knees to do anything but follow him down to the lobby and outside the building. Gulping in the fresh air, she turned to him and said, "Why is it, Charlie Whitman, that I'm never entirely sure if I should kiss you or kill you?"

Charlie's eyes danced. "Let me help you answer that."

He leaned in, his mouth slanting over hers; she held him off, a hand at his chest. "Why'd you do it, Charlie? Why did you tell Vince it was my idea?"

He shrugged. "Why not?"

Studying him, she tilted her head. "That was a nice thing to do." She was beginning to suspect there was more to Charlie Whitman than met the eye, and she had to admit, she liked what she saw . . . a lot.

It *was* a nice thing to do, Charlie thought. So nice, it was totally out of character. For a minute, it made him nervous. This lady with her taffy-colored hair and bright blue eyes could be dangerous. Pretending to glance around, he hushed her. "Quiet, Cassie Armstrong. I have my reputation to consider."

She laughed. "Well, thank you."

"You're welcome." He smiled at her. "So, where would you like to go to celebrate, tonight? After all, the world is your oyster. It's not every day you beat out someone like Vince Bertolli."

Some of the light left her eyes. "I'm sorry. I can't. I already have a date."

His eyes danced. "Break it."

When Cassie shook her head, Charlie smiled, a little ruefully this time. "You really are a woman of principle, Armstrong. Just when I think I'm making a true advertising executive out of you, those damned principles of yours keep getting in the way."

Her smile, too, was a little rueful. "Can I take a rain check?"

He smiled at her. "I'll try to fit you in." And then he grinned, removing three sheets of paper from his back pocket. "Well, I guess we won't be needing these anymore."

"The concepts! You really did write them."

"Well, of course, Armstrong. I may be outrageous, but I am not totally crazy."

As he ripped them up into tiny pieces, Cassie laughed. Charlie Whitman was outrageous, she thought, outrageous and nice. Giving in to impulse, she stood on tiptoe to brush a light kiss against his cheek. "Thank you, Charlie," she whispered, and then she was gone.

Charlie Whitman, sophisticated man of the world, stared after her, a hand raised to his cheek.

FLUSHED WITH VICTORY, she was still laughing that evening at dinner as she regaled Jeff Paulson with the events of her day.

"He sounds like quite a guy," Jeff admitted as they lingered over dessert.

"Character is more like it," Cassie corrected, sipping her coffee.

"He certainly must be, since you haven't talked about anything else all night."

Coffee cup at her lips, Cassie colored slightly. Jeff was right. She had talked about nothing but Charlie Whitman all through dinner. "Oh, Jeff, I'm sorry. And I didn't even ask you how your lecture went today."

"No problem," he told her with a quiet smile, and proceeded to tell her about his symposium.

Jeff Paulson was a nice man, well mannered, considerate, scholarly. A professor of English at City College. They'd met almost eight months ago when Cassie started teaching a night course there. They had a lot in common—common interests, a similar sense of humor. And he was very attractive, too, in a conservative, understated way, with his lanky blond hair and hazel eyes that smiled quietly at her from behind the rims of his wire-framed glasses. She should have been head over heels in love, yet when Jeff kissed her at the end of the night and asked to come into her apartment, she found herself telling him no.

It wasn't sheer prudery that made her refuse. She wasn't waiting for a wedding ring. She'd even had a lover in college. She liked Jeff Paulson, she liked him a lot, but she wasn't committed to him yet, or to this relationship, and she wasn't going to go any further until she was. No, she thought, it was probably a case of those damned principles of hers getting in the way again. She could just hear Charlie Whitman laugh at that. And then right on its heels came another, even more confusing thought. Why, oh, why was she thinking of Charlie Whitman?

3

"MEN ARE SLIME," a husky female voice announced dramatically. Conference report forgotten, Cassie looked up from behind her desk. Had the voice belonged to anyone besides Fran Gorham, she might have been alarmed. Instead, long inured to Fran's theatrical style, she merely smiled. Wearing a hot-pink designer minidress that clashed pleasantly with her vibrant auburn hair, Fran plopped herself down in Cassie's office without an invitation—but then she rarely bothered with the conventional trappings.

By some strange attraction of opposites, Cassie Armstrong and Fran Gorham were the best of friends and had been ever since they'd first laid eyes on one another. Cassie had served as Fran's summer intern during New York University's program matching up graduating students with seasoned alumni. Armed with her degree in English, Cassie had decided to summer in advertising as a lark before she returned home to teach at the local high school. It had been Fran who'd convinced her to stay on at Woodson & Meyers, and Cassie could never quite decide whether to thank Fran or murder her for that fate-altering advice.

Although only two years older than Cassie, Fran had been born aged thirty-five-plus, or so she claimed. She was the only child of a successful advertising executive father whose exploits were widely known and gleefully haled in the affluent Westchester suburb where she'd grown up. Fran's mother kept herself too busy with Junior League teas and spending Mr. Gorham's money to notice her husband was a philanderer. As a result, Fran was the quintessential New York yuppie—brittle-edged, hard of heart and deep down, very lonely.

"So," Cassie said. "Are we discussing one man in particular or the whole sex in general?"

"Grady Harriman in particular," Fran replied succinctly. "But if the shoe fits . . ."

"Oh, Lord," Cassie groaned. "Fran, you didn't. You didn't finally agree to go out with him, did you?" A vice president in account services, slick was the first, last and middle adjective that came to mind when describing Grady, which of course explained his spectacular success in the advertising business. He'd been after Fran since day one.

Fran grimaced. "Worse. That sleaze bag stood me up. Said something better came along. And since Grady has *GQ* looks but the IQ of this desk, that undoubtedly means someone not yet old enough to vote. Do you believe it?"

No, Cassie didn't. Not only because Fran was beautiful in that chic, New York trendy way that Cassie so admired but didn't dare emulate for fear she'd look like she'd dressed up in her older sister's clothes, but also because of Fran's knifelike anger. It was rumored around the agency that Fran's mouth was registered with the police department as a lethal weapon. Deep down, Cassie knew her friend was a really nice person, just as she knew Fran hid that vulnerable side of herself from the world. Fran deserved better than Grady Harriman. Every woman deserved better than Grady Harriman. "Hey, Fran, I'm sorry."

Her friend waved it aside. "Serves me right for agreeing to go out with that blow-dried mannequin in the first place. I think I'm giving up on dating. I'm tired of going out with men whose favorite game is 'mirror, mirror on the wall, who's the prettiest one of all? Ooh, what a surprise—me!'"

Even as Cassie protested, she had to laugh. "Come on, Fran. It's not that bad. There are nice men left in this world."

Fran raised a skeptical brow. "Like who?"

At the challenge, Cassie sighed. This was not exactly a new game. "Well, there's Jeff. Jeff's a nice person."

"Okay," Fran conceded. "I'll agree with you there. Jeff Paulson is nice."

"And there's Joe. Joe Mancini is nice. You have to give me that one."

A long pause ensued. "You're right," Fran agreed quietly. "Joe is nice."

And Charlie Whitman? Cassie didn't dare voice the thought. She already knew Fran's answer to that one. "You see. That's two nice men already. There's somebody out there for you, Fran. You just haven't found him yet."

"That's the problem with talking to you, Cassie. You're always so cheery and positive. It's downright unnatural. Not to mention depressing." Fran crossed her long legs. "Speaking of Jeff, are you going out with the good professor tonight?"

Cassie shook her head. "He's attending a lecture on the 'English Romantics and their effect on the human context.' That's a direct quote, by the way."

Fran's amber eyes widened. "Now there's somebody with an IQ higher than a gnat. I don't even know what that means."

"I'm not sure I do, either," Cassie confessed with a grin. "He invited me along, but I don't know. Somehow the idea of a lecture seems a little dull for a Friday night."

"What's the matter with these men?" Fran grumbled. "They're either too smart or too stupid for their own good. So, I guess this means it's you and me, kid. We could go to some elegant Upper East Side winery and cruise for Mr. Right, or we could go back to my place and quietly commit suicide. At the present moment, the suicide route seems the least painful."

"*Casablanca*'s on tonight," Cassie offered. "We could pick up some ice cream."

"Oh, good. We can eat until we're too fat to date. Perfect. Who needs men, anyway?"

As if on cue, a tall figure with curly brown hair and lively gray eyes stood in the doorway. "Excuse me, is this male-bashing session private or can anyone join in?"

At the mere sight of him, Cassie smiled. By now, Charlie Whitman's T-shirt collection was legendary around the agency. Today he was resplendently attired in one that read Catch A Wave Gumby, complete with a tiny green man riding a fluorescent pink surfboard. Fran, of course, had a slightly different reaction.

"Oh, God." She shot up her hands in disgust. "The end to a perfect day. Now my evening really is complete. Well, well, well, it's a small world, Charlie Whitman."

"And getting smaller all the time," he countered readily.

Fran eyed him, one brow arched. "Well, Charlie, you're like a bad penny. Long time, no see. Jump ship again?"

"Fran, if I'd known you were here, I might have gone down with the *Titanic*."

"I'd introduce you two," Cassie said, "but it seems like time-out is more in order." She knew they were already acquainted. It had been Fran who'd given her the lowdown on Charlie before he'd started at the agency.

"My little bird," she informed Charlie with a grin.

Well, well, well, Charlie thought, *another little surprise from Ms. Cassie Armstrong. Fran and Cassie, friends. Who would have thunk it?* He turned to Fran. "Aha, so you're the one who slandered my good name. I should have guessed. Charlie I'll-Try-Anything-for-a-Year Whitman." And then he grinned. "Not bad, Fran. For the Mouth of Madison."

"The Mouth of Madison . . . Why, you. . . ."

Beneath their cynical banter, Cassie heard the unspoken bond of two survivors of the advertising wars. They might not love one another, but they grudgingly respected each other's talents, which were considerable. In her own inimitable way, Fran was every bit as good as Charlie.

"Well, ladies, much as I'd love to stay and sling insults, it is Friday night and duty calls. And speaking of which, I don't suppose I could tempt you with a friendly beer at Cronin's." Though he addressed both of them, his eyes singled Cassie out.

Cassie hesitated. She wanted to go, probably more than was smart or wise. But being a loyal person, her first allegiance was to her friend. And Fran, very decisively, let her feelings be known.

"Drop dead, Whitman," she drawled. "We have better things to do. Besides, you're wasting your time. Cassie's already got a boyfriend."

"Sorry," Cassie added quietly. "Fran and I have plans."

Was it three or four times now that she'd turned him down? Charlie hadn't kept track. *Face it, Whitman, though you might be irresistible, the woman is managing to resist.* It was not his usual style to pursue an unwilling woman, not when there were so many willing ones, but something about Cassie Armstrong made him keep coming back for more. He wondered where the good boyfriend was tonight, but didn't dare ask in front of Fran. "Ah, well, ladies, my heart is broken, so I guess this only leaves me with work." He handed several sheets across the desk. "Your copy, Armstrong . . . wouldn't want you to worry about it all weekend or send out the mounted police after me or anything like that."

"And only a week late," she cried out happily. "You're doing better and better."

Fran cast Charlie a look that could have sliced the flesh from a lesser man. "He's not giving you any problems, is he?"

"Well . . ." Cassie hedged. "Define problems."

"Because if you are, Charlie Whitman, you are going to have to answer to me."

"Oh, no, oh, no," Charlie cried out in falsetto. "Not that. I'll take the rack, drawing and quartering . . . but not the Mouth. I will be good. Oh, I will be good."

Fran slung back, "Whitman, have you ever considered professional therapy? Because I know orangutans who are more together than you."

"So are we into orangutans these days, Fran? I heard about old Grady standing you up."

Cassie threw up her hands. "Enough, you two. Enough."

"The voice of reason prevails," Charlie said with a smile for Cassie. "If you have any questions about the copy, either Joe or I—" Charlie looked around, noticed Joe's absence from the group. "Now where is my silent partner?" With an exasperated sigh, he spotted the other man out in the hall. "Oh, Joe, come on in here. I told you they don't bite." He shot a glance at Cassie. "Pull hair maybe, bite no." He all but dragged Joe into the room. "Say hi to the ladies, Joe. Come on, this will only hurt for a minute."

Joe shifted his weight uneasily, nodded at Cassie, then looked Fran straight in the eye. "Hi, Fran. How are you?"

"Hi, Joe." Fran smiled slightly. "I haven't seen you in a while."

It was a perfectly normal exchange, a routine greeting between two people who worked at the same agency. And that was precisely what bothered Charlie and Cassie. Cornflower blue eyes snapped to lively gray ones, and the cogs churned, two great minds thinking as one.

Was it possible? Charlie's eyes asked.

Could it be? Cassie's answered.

Fran, the Mouth of Madison, and Joe, the ever-silent silent partner?

It was impossible. And yet . . .

At the risk of having his face rearranged, Charlie decided to test out their hypothesis. "I don't suppose I could persuade you ladies to change your plans and join Joe and me tonight, could I?"

"Well, I don't know," Cassie demurred. "I'm game, but . . . Fran, what do you say?"

For the first time since Cassie had known her, the brazen Fran refused to meet her eye. She stared at the floor as if she'd just discovered her shoes, trendy hot-pink numbers that were strangely at odds with her hesitant tone when she answered. "Well, sure . . . I suppose. I mean . . . if that's okay with you, Joe?"

"Okay!" Joe replied without hesitation. "That would be great."

"Do you believe it?" Cassie asked Charlie when Fran and Joe left to get their coats. "Fran and Joe? I would never have put those two together. I mean, they're so different."

"Sounds like ninety-nine point nine percent of all couples to me."

"Spoken like a true cynic."

Those gray eyes smiled at her, full of lazy humor. "Opposites attract, Armstrong. Haven't you figured that out yet?"

She tilted her head and looked at him, her heart thudding unevenly in her chest. "Oh, really?"

"I have it on the best authority."

"And just who might that be?"

He grinned at her. "Why, Oprah, of course."

"Of course. And you're probably the only man around the agency who has time to watch 'Oprah.'"

"I always take time for what's important."

As she picked up her coat, Cassie suddenly had second thoughts. "I don't know about this, Charlie. We're matchmaking. This is terrible."

Sighing, he helped her on with her coat. "Lighten up, Armstrong."

"Grow up, Whitman. I mean, suppose we're wrong about Fran and Joe."

"Well, then—" he grinned at her "—I suppose we'll have our first date."

The thudding sensation was back, in spades. "This isn't a date," she reminded him.

A teasing glint entered his eyes. "You're right. It's a mission. A cause. We're helping out two friends, buddies in arms. It's noble, self-sacrificing. My God, it's got your name written all over it."

She picked up her purse. "Are you going to tease me all night?"

"Probably. You got a problem with that?"

"No. Just like to know what to expect."

And so did he, for that matter. He pressed the elevator button. "So where's the boyfriend tonight, Armstrong?"

"At a lecture." Stepping inside the empty car, she wanted to explain about Jeff, but wasn't quite sure how to without sounding like an idiot. After all, as she herself had pointed out, this wasn't exactly a date.

He eyed her in surprise. "A lecture? On a Friday night? Sounds like a serious guy."

"He is." She fiddled with her purse strap; she didn't want to talk about Jeff Paulson, except Charlie wouldn't let the topic go.

"So, what does he do?"

She sighed. "He's a professor."

"Of?"

"English." Charlie's eyes demanded more. "At City College. He has a Ph.D. His name is Jeff Paulson. And he owns a small house on Long Island. I don't know the appraised value, but I'll get back to you. And why are you so interested in him?"

Charlie arched a brow. "Why are you so defensive? He's your boyfriend."

"He is not my boyfriend," she snapped, sounding every bit as defensive as he'd accused her of being. "He's just someone I go out with, okay?" There. It was out. Afraid she'd given too much away, she immediately turned the tables on him. "And you're the one who doesn't like labels, Charlie Whitman. So why are you putting a label on this?"

The elevator doors slid open, saving him a reply, but as they joined the others he favored her with a speculative gleam. "On to Cronin's," he announced gaily.

"On to Cronin's," she echoed, but she'd caught his look. What had she done now?

ANYONE WHO ASSOCIATED meat markets with Chicago had never patronized Cronin's, Third Avenue, New York. A popular advertising hangout, the bar lived up to its reputation this Friday night. As Charlie held open the door, allowing the two women to precede him, every head in the place swiveled as if in choreographed action. At the sight of two unescorted females under the age of ninety, several liquor-emboldened cruisers cruised forward, then stepped back in disappointment when Charlie and Joe entered on their heels.

"What a bunch of lowlifes," Charlie observed with cheerful disdain, "trying to pick up women in a bar. I'm ashamed to be a man."

"Right, Whitman," Cassie shouted above the din. "As if you haven't done the exact same thing yourself."

He leaned closer to whisper in her ear. "There you go, Armstrong. I'll have you know I've never even been in this place."

A bearded man stepped past them, stopping to tap Charlie on the arm. "Hey, Charlie. Good to see you back here, buddy. You enjoy the game last night?" When Cassie laughed, Charlie looked at her. "All right. Maybe once or twice. So what are you drinking, Armstrong?" Those gray eyes twinkled. "Sloe gin fizz? Shirley Temple? Oh, no, I've got it. White wine spritzer. The perfect uptown-girl drink."

Her eyes held a glint. "Make it a Michelob and hold the glass."

"Well, all right, Armstrong. Now we're talking." He turned to the other two to get their drink orders, then led Joe toward the bar, leaving the two women alone.

Fran pounced. "You set me up, Cassandra Elaine Armstrong. And don't bother to deny it," she added when she saw the guilty look in Cassie's eyes. "You could never lie worth a damn, anyway."

"You're right," Cassie confessed. "Fran, I'm sorry. I know I shouldn't have, but . . . I don't know. It seemed like a good idea at the time. It's that damned Charlie Whitman. He's always getting me into trouble. Are you very mad at me?"

"Mad at you?" Fran grinned. "I could kiss you."

Cassie blinked. "You mean you really like Joe?"

"Yeah." Fran nodded. "I really think I do. He's so different. He's so . . ."

Opposites attract, Cassie thought, staring at the bar, and one man with curly brown hair in particular. A crowd had gathered around him, and she watched as they threw back their heads and roared at one of Charlie's remarks.

"So shy, so sweet . . ." Fran's voice trailed off as she caught Cassie's distracted look. Debating whether to mind her own business, she forwent tact in favor of friendship. "He's the life of the party, isn't he?"

"Yes," Cassie agreed. And then she realized they were not discussing Joe Mancini now.

Fran eyed her significantly. "He always is. Too bad he isn't so good the morning after the party. So what's going on between you and Charlie Whitman?"

"I— What do you mean? Nothing. We work together, that's—"

"Trying to lie again, Cassandra?" her friend asked, not unkindly. "Auntie Fran always knows better."

And she always did. "I don't know," Cassie admitted with a sigh. "I don't know what's going on. That's the truth."

"That's just what I was afraid of," Fran muttered. "Look, Cassie, deep down, I like Charlie Whitman, but—"

"Fran, this really isn't necessary."

Fran held up her hand. "Just hear me out, okay?"

Cassie nodded slowly.

"I admit that even I had a crush on him back in my salad days." When Cassie's eyes widened, she hastily added, "Oh, don't worry. Nothing happened. Nothing ever does with Charlie Whitman. That's the point. Oh, sure, he can show a girl a heck of a good time, and I'm sure you're flattered by all the attention. Charlie's a hell of a catch. Even I'll concede that. But, honey..."

"I already know what you're going to say, Fran. You're going to tell me that he's not my type. That Charlie Whitman will never stick around and that I shouldn't take him seriously. I should stick with nice guys like Jeff. I know all that. But, Fran, can't I just have fun?"

"Sure, Cassie, sure. It's just that... Well, it's just that I don't want to see you get hurt, that's all."

"And I won't," Cassie promised.

Fran sighed. "I just hope you're right." She looked beyond Cassie. "They're coming back with the drinks."

"Well, we were right about Fran and Joe," she told Charlie when Fran and Joe wandered off toward the back of the bar. "She likes him."

"And he's crazy about her. We make quite a team, Armstrong." Lounging negligently against a center island, he held out his hand in her direction. "Put her there, partner."

Even a simple handshake in the middle of a crowded room caused the electricity that always existed between them to flash to life. Startled, she tried to pull back, but smiling at her, Charlie refused to let her go. He toyed with her fingers one by one, causing her skin to prickle and heat at his touch.

Reminding herself that she was not a woman to melt lightly, Cassie swallowed hard. "I hope it works out with Fran and Joe. Fran deserves it. She's a nice person."

Smiling faintly at the small blush on her face, Charlie laughed into those serious eyes. "I can think of many adjectives to describe Fran Gorham, but nice is not among them."

"No, she is, Charlie. She's helped me out a lot."

"You seem to bring out the best in people, Armstrong." And he should know. For all her seriousness, he liked this woman, couldn't help liking her. And that scared him a little, more than a little.

She met his eyes. "Maybe that's just because I see the best in them."

"Oh, yeah?" Almost absently, he entwined her hand in his, causing her pulse to rocket. "So what do you see in me?"

She saw a lot, but not wanting to give herself away, she laughed. "I'm still working on that one."

"Aha. Now why do I get the funny feeling that Fran has warned you about my less-than-sterling character?"

"How'd you guess?"

"I know Fran," he responded dryly. "So what did she tell you, that I'm a cross between Peter Pan, Bluebeard and Casanova?"

"Something like that."

"I suppose this is the perfect opportunity to deny it all, but what can I say, Armstrong." He wanted her to know the score. "Fran's a smart woman."

It was an oddly serious conversation to be having in the middle of a fun-filled bar with a man who was rarely serious. But then Charlie Whitman rarely did what she expected. She supposed that was what she liked about him. "Are you warning me off, too, Charlie?"

He had to laugh at that. "I suppose I am."

If anything, that only made her like him more. And she couldn't help but tease him back a little. "And here I thought you had no principles. Maybe instead of you rubbing off on me, I'm rubbing off on you."

Those gray eyes sparkled. "Perish the thought. You mean I'm turning into a nice person? I'll have to start helping little old ladies across the street, doing good deeds for friends. My God, next year I'll probably end up heading the agency Christmas dance. Oh, please, shoot me now and put me out of my misery."

Pulling her hand out of his, she tried to punch him in the shoulder, but he readily thwarted her, grasping her hand firmly. "I don't think so, Armstrong. With my luck one of those brothers of yours is probably the golden gloves champ of upstate." He put his drink down on the island, matching her smile with one of his own. "So what do you say, Armstrong? You want to have fun with no labels on it?"

"I put myself in the hands of the master."

"Then come on. Drink up. I know the perfect place to get our shy little friends together."

4

"A POOL HALL!" Cassie exclaimed as the foursome climbed out of the taxi. "You're taking us to a pool hall?" She didn't know why she was so surprised. As the cab had whizzed downtown under Charlie's direction and as the passing neighborhoods had grown less and less gentrified, it would not have taken a Nobel Prize winner to have figured out that Charlie was hatching some devious plan. By now, Cassie had come to dread and anticipate that mischievous sparkle in those gray eyes. "Charlie Whitman, have you taken total leave of your senses?"

"Relax, Armstrong," he drawled for her ears only. "This place is just the ticket. If played correctly, pool requires a minimum of talking and a maximum of body contact. Perfect for my shy little friend. Trust me."

She supposed she'd have to. But one look at Fran's designer miniskirt and the dismayed disdain that crossed her face as she stepped inside the threshold made Cassie question the wisdom of Charlie's ways. The interior of Rex's Pool Parlor was even less prepossessing than its shabby exterior, a thing Cassie wouldn't have thought possible. The harsh glare of fluorescent lights competed against a hazy cloud of stale smoke, illuminating a scene that might have come straight out of the honky-tonk pool halls of *The Hustler*. Fortunately for them, the cavernous converted warehouse was nearly empty on this Friday night, but one look at her fellow occupants had Cassie eyeing the exit longingly. Even the normally stoic Joe appeared shell-shocked.

Nevertheless, when Charlie seated them around a scarred pine table with ill-matching chairs, Cassie tried to be a good sport. "Well, this place is certainly very... unpretentious."

"Oh, it's that all right," Fran agreed, trying to remain pleasant, but losing the battle as acidity crept into her tone. "I've often wanted to socialize with Hell's Angels. Thank you so much, Charlie, for making a lifelong dream come true."

Following the direction of Fran's gaze, Cassie noticed two gentlemen with sixties-style long hair, bearded faces and black leather vests. As the burly one of the two flexed his heavily muscled arm to line up his shot, a tattoo of a snake slithered and twisted. Cassie could only stare. "They do look like Hell's Angels. You don't think..." Misinterpreting her interest, Snake winked at her; Cassie quickly looked back to her own group.

"Ladies, ladies," Charlie broke in, "you've got to give this place a chance. Rex's is an acquired taste. It has to grow on you. Like caviar, a good cigar, a fine wine..."

"Or fungus," Fran snapped, shooting Charlie a look that would have had a less stalwart soul pushing up daisies.

Charlie sighed. "I think drinks are in order here. Many drinks." He turned to Joe. "Shall we head over to the bar?"

"Hurry back," Cassie urged, unsure which made her more nervous, the impending wrath of Fran or her newfound friend, Snake.

"I'm out of here," Fran announced the minute Joe and Charlie were out of hearing distance. "I, of all people, should have known better than to trust Charlie Whitman's judgment. What's he going to do for his finale, have us sipping Thunderbird in the Bowery?"

Cassie grabbed her arm and pulled her down into the chair. "Come on, Fran. It's not that bad. Where's your spirit of adventure?"

"Somewhere back on the Upper East Side. Which is exactly where I plan to be as soon as I rescue Joe and hail a cab. Not that you can find a cab in this seedy neighborhood. Coming?"

"No, and neither are you." Grabbing Fran's minuscule purse—the latest in trendy New York fashion— away from her, she planted it firmly on the table. "Live dangerously, I always say."

Fran's eyes narrowed. "You have never said anything remotely like that, Cassie Armstrong, in the entire six years I've known you. What's gotten into you tonight?"

"Nothing. Can't I just have fun?" But at the knowing look on her friend's face, she deliberately changed the subject. "So how's it going with Joe?"

The diversionary tactic worked. A softer look crept over Fran's face. "Good. At least I think good. I'm just not sure how to act around him. He's so shy, so different."

"Just be yourself, Fran," Cassie advised and then she corrected herself. "Your nice self. The person that I know exists deep down under all that sophistication."

"I don't want to get hurt, Cassie. I don't want to make a fool of myself. God knows, I saw a lifetime of that with my parents. I don't want to end up like my mother."

Cassie reached across the table and squeezed Fran's hand. "You won't, Fran. Joe's one of the good guys. You know that. And he likes you. Charlie told me, and he wouldn't lie about a thing like that. Joe won't hurt you, Fran. But you've got to give him a chance. You've got to let him get to know you—the real you."

Fran expelled a deep puff of air, then managed a shaky smile. "I know. Except I'm so nervous. My God, I'm thirty-two years old and I feel like this is my first date."

Fran wasn't the only one who was nervous. Across the pool hall a similar conversation was taking place.

Charlie laid a big, brotherly hand on Joe's massive shoulder. "Relax, buddy. She likes you. You're in like Flynn. Got it made in the shade. And I got it from an unimpeachable source—the best friend! It's the time-honored seventh-grade system. Just remember, use nouns, verbs, sentences and whenever possible throw in an adjective or adverb or two."

Joe pleaded for mercy with his eyes.

"Okay, forget that, big guy. You'll have to settle for the strong-but-silent type. Now, come on, let's go. The ladies are waiting."

Operation Matchmaking appeared to have stalled before it had begun. As the foursome sipped their drinks, the advice and the liquor seemed wasted. A disquieting silence fell over the table, one not even Cassie and Charlie could break. When the conversation came down to the weather, Cassie knew they were in deep trouble. *Come on, Fran, talk!* Cassie urged with her eyes. But the usually voluble Fran seemed turned to stone. And Joe proved his usual helpful self in the ice-breaking department.

"Well." Charlie sighed into the abyss. "Enough small talk. Why don't we play a little pool? Fran, have you ever played before?"

"Ah ... no."

Perfect, thought Charlie, as he led them to an empty table. "Well, Joe, how about if you take Fran for your partner and Cassie and I will team up. Joe," he directed, "show Fran how to hold the cue."

Hopeless, Charlie decided as he watched Joe very patiently and earnestly try to explain in words what Fran was supposed do. "I said *show* her, Joe. Like this ..." Maneuvering Joe's body behind Fran, Charlie pushed him close.

A light bulb flicked on over Joe Mancini's head. "Oh ... like this."

Better, Charlie thought with quiet satisfaction, *much better*. Turning to the smiling Cassie, he moved deliberately toward her. "Now, Armstrong. This is how the game is played." When he was close enough, he whispered in her ear. "What did I tell you? A little enforced body contact. Works like a charm. Ready for your lesson?"

Laughing at him, she stepped back. "Forget it, Whitman. I already know how to play. I've got three brothers, remember? Shall we rack 'em up?"

It soon became evident that the teams were hopelessly misaligned. To nobody's great surprise, Charlie was an excellent player. It was Cassie who shocked them all.

Well, well, well, Charlie thought, watching Cassie effortlessly knock two balls into a corner pocket. Another surprise from the demure Ms. Armstrong. "You didn't tell me you were a hustler, lady."

Leaning across the table, she squinted one eye as she lined up her next shot. "I grew up in Upstate New York, remember? There's not much to do there in the winter."

Charlie and Cassie quickly demolished the other two. But that was beside the point. Laughing over all her inept mistakes, Fran was a far cry from her usually sophisticated, cynical self, and Joe, in his element, took every opportunity to help her with her shots.

"I give up," Fran declared at last, dropping her cue on the table with a clatter. "I am absolutely hopeless at this game."

Joe was quick to console her. "No, no. You did great. Really."

"Do you really think so?"

In answer, Joe tentatively reached out to touch her. A look of pure rapture crossed over his face when Fran met him halfway, sliding her hand into his. As Joe led her toward a quiet corner, Fran glanced at Cassie and Charlie. "I think we'll take a break now."

At her breathless tone, Charlie met Cassie's eye, a triumphant look on his face. "What did I tell you, Armstrong? There's a method to my madness."

"A sneaky and devious plan." Cassie shook her head admiringly. "Some might call you a con artist, Charlie Whitman."

"Thank you. So what do you say, Armstrong? You ready to take on the master? I warn you, when I play I take no prisoners. Girl or no girl."

With a glint in her eye, she replied, "A little eight ball, perhaps? Name your poison, Whitman. Whatever you can play, I can play better."

"Oh, ho. Aren't we the cocky one tonight. All right then, lady, eight ball's the name of the game. And just to make the competition a little more interesting, what do you say we place a small wager on it?"

She met the challenge in his eyes with one of her own. "Loser buys the drinks?"

He shook his head. "That is dull, unimaginative and exactly what I'd expect from someone in account management. Come on, Armstrong, not afraid you're going to lose, are you?"

"The thought never crossed my mind. All right then, how about, if I win, you finish all your assignments on time and—" she finished with a flourish "—all without any nagging from me."

"You drive a hard bargain, lady. But all right."

"And if you win? Not that that will ever happen, of course."

He didn't even have to think about it. "A date. You go out with me for one night, Armstrong. All alone, no best friends, no chaperons."

The thudding sensation was in her heart. "Well, gee, Charlie, I don't know. I mean, I don't usually go out with men who are Peter Pan, Bluebeard and Casanova all rolled into one."

"Sorry, my terms are not negotiable. That's the deal, Armstrong. Take it or leave it."

"Rack 'em up, Whitman." She chalked her cue. "And prepare to meet your maker."

Charlie won the break, then proceeded to make his next four shots.

"Luck," Cassie scoffed. "Pure beginner's luck."

"What can I tell you, Armstrong? I'm motivated."

He also seemed to have the angles on his side. The game was almost over before it began until, finally, he missed a shot. At long last, it was Cassie's turn, except he hadn't left her any good angles. And those mischievous eyes of his hardly helped. She made her first shot, but just barely, causing Charlie to lean in close. "Not trying to throw this game, are you, Armstrong?"

"No." Elbowing him lightly in the ribs, she pushed him back. "And stop trying to distract me."

"If only it was that easy."

She played valiantly, but he played better, finishing off the last ball, then turning to face her with a grin. "Too bad, Armstrong. You lose."

She tried to look disappointed. "Best two out of three?"

"No way." Removing the cue from her hand, he placed it in the rack. "I won, fair and square. Tomorrow night. Your place. Seven o'clock. Be there. And prepare for a night you'll always remember."

"It's a shame you're not more confident," she began, then stopped. "I can't make it tomorrow night, Charlie."

"Sorry, I'm not accepting a previous date as an excuse. You'll just have to break it."

"No, it's not a date. My brother is graduating from high school this weekend and my parents planned a big party on Sunday. We're having all these guests from out of town." For an instant, she debated inviting him along, then changed her mind. It was too soon, and Charlie didn't exactly strike her as the hearth-and-home type. Besides, she wasn't entirely sure what they'd make of him, either. Charlie Whitman was an acquired taste, like caviar, a fine wine, or even, she added with a grin, fungus. "I'm sorry, Charlie, I just can't miss it. It would break their hearts if I wasn't there."

He wasn't sure what bothered him most, that he was being turned down yet again—for a brother's graduation, no less—or that she came from a family who celebrated these things. Or maybe what bothered him most was that he didn't. His parents had been in Europe vacationing when he'd graduated. Their absence had not surprised him; they rarely even remembered his birthday, and if they did, they honored it with a check—no card, just a check.

At the expression on his face, she stopped. "You don't believe me, do you?"

"Oh, no, it's not that. Nobody could make up an excuse like that." He forced his head to clear. "So which brother is it? You have three, if I recall. Is this the hair puller? The pool hustler?"

She laughed, shaking her head. "No, my youngest brother, Timmy." She grinned at the thought of her brother, who had red hair and freckles and was always into everything. "I think he might have been an accident, since he's five years younger than my sister, but my parents aren't talking."

Accidents happened in the best of homes, Charlie thought, or even in the worst, such as his own.

He led her to their table, smiling at the sight of Fran and Joe locked together on the dance floor and oblivious to the world. "So tell me about your childhood," he invited.

"There's not much to tell, really." She sipped at her beer. "It was an ordinary, uneventful childhood, as childhoods go. I grew up the oldest of five children."

"Which is why you're the serious, overly conscientious person that you are."

"Conscientious," she corrected. "Anyway, there's me, then my brother Frank, Jr. He's married, with three kids, and works with my dad at the hardware store. Then there's Thomas. He still lives in Kingston, and he's a pharmacist. He and his wife have one child. Then there's my sister, Cathy. She's married to a state trooper and pregnant with her first. And then there's Timmy. No wife in the offing yet, but tons of girlfriends."

Charlie smiled. "Small town, of course?"

"Not that small," she defended her place of birth. "Kingston just happens to be world-renowned as the gateway to Upstate New York. Not to mention that it's strategically located on the New York Thruway."

"Sorry, I must have missed that one on my world tour. So how'd you end up in the city?"

"For my Master's program. I did my undergraduate work at SUNY Albany, which is fairly close to home, so I guess I was ready to test my wings a little and try out the bright lights of the Big Apple. When NYU offered me a partial scholarship, I grabbed it. My father is still recovering from the shock. He personally installed three locks on my apartment door. I think he really believes muggers lurk around every corner."

"He's not entirely wrong. And that explains everything about you, except how you ended up working in an advertising agency."

"Ah, that one's easy." She explained it in one word. "Fran. I was her summer intern, and she wouldn't exactly take no for an answer."

"Sounds like the Gorham we all know and love." He glanced at the barely moving pair in the center of the room, smiling at their star-struck expressions. *To Fran,* he thought, with a mental toast of his beer.

"And how is it, Charlie Whitman, that you now know everything there is to know about me, but I know absolutely nothing about you?"

He slugged down his beer before replying airily, "Oh, I had your ordinary, uneventful childhood, as childhoods go."

Cassie took a sip of beer and studied him. "Why do I find that hard to believe?"

He didn't want to talk about it. No surprise there. He never did.

"Come on, Charlie. *I* told *you.* You're not going to make me interview you, are you?"

Recognizing that determined look on her face, he realized she probably would, but then she had no idea of the Pandora's box she was opening. He sighed. "What can I tell you, Armstrong? I'm an only child. I grew up in New York—the city that is, not the 'burbs. I summered in Connecticut, where all New Yorkers of a certain status go in the summer, like lemmings to the sea. I was kicked out of the hallowed halls of no less than four prep schools before one dubious institution conceded to graduate me. I think my parents bribed them, but I have no proof, of course. All the headmasters agreed that I was exceedingly bright, but that I failed to apply myself and that I had a tendency to be a bad influence on my fellow students. Can you imagine, Armstrong, anyone saying such a thing about me?"

She laughed. "I'm still trying to imagine you as a preppie. So you're one of those rich Eastern seaboard establishment types I'm always reading about?"

"Sorry to disappoint you, but I've managed to get myself disinherited without a sou, for which I am eternally grateful."

Something about his brittle tone caused the laughter to leave her eyes. "And your parents?"

"Ah, yes, the parents." He filled his glass and took a hefty swig before replying. "Well, what can one say about Sylvia and Charles Bennington Whitman, the Third?" Actually, he thought, the less said the better. "They're both psychiatrists, very successful if one classifies success in terms of money and material possessions, which they do. My father is a Freudian and my mother is a behavioral Skinnerian, which probably explains why I was not potty trained until I was ten. They married late in life, had me later, and I believe my advent in the world was the biggest shock of their lives. You'd think two people who'd graduated from medical school might have managed to grasp the simple facts of life, but then dear old Mom and Dad are not big believers in reality." Or kindness either; they'd never let him forget the accident of his birth. But he couldn't tell Cassie that. "In terms of marital stability," he continued, keeping it factual, "they could rival Burton and Taylor. They've been married, divorced, then remarried, with countless separations and reconciliations in between. I think they're still married, but then it's been twenty minutes since I spoke to them, so I'm not really sure."

Though there was nothing remotely funny about what he'd said, she laughed, mostly because he seemed to expect it.

"Oh, that's not the funny part," he told her. "The funny part is they think I need analysis." They'd also had their fair share of custody battles, but old Charles and Sylvia seemed to get a little confused in that department. They'd both tried to give him away. For one instant, he was that eight-year-old boy again, but he wouldn't think of that now. There were some things not even Charlie Whitman could joke about. Instead, he drew a deep breath. "So what can I tell you, Armstrong? My childhood wasn't 'The Brady Bunch.' It wasn't even 'Married . . . With Children.' And if you're saying to yourself, aha, now I understand him, you'd probably be right. I am a hopeless flirt, I never take anything seriously and I avoid any and all commitment like the plague. In short, I'm probably the worst kind of guy for you. In fact, I'm sure that protective father of yours would be horrified to know you were even talking to me. And you know something? He'd probably be right."

Although he'd held a lot back, he'd said more to Cassie Armstrong than he'd said to any other woman, any other person. In the aftermath, he found himself strangely relieved and more than slightly embarrassed. Sipping at his beer, he couldn't bring himself to meet her eyes. "See, Armstrong, your ordinary, run-of-the-mill childhood."

But Cassie saw behind the flippant words, sensed the pain beneath. Her hand crept to his. "I don't know, Charlie. I still think you're kind of nice."

"Nice! Nice?" He sighed heavily, shaking his head. "Haven't you heard a word I've said? There you go again, Armstrong, thinking the best of people. How many times do I have to warn you about that?"

"What's wrong with that?" she challenged.

"You can get hurt," Charlie told her. "In fact, it's guaranteed."

"I guess that's the risk you have to take. It's called living, Charlie Whitman." And how strange that she should be telling him about risks.

"Spoken like someone who's never gotten hurt. And how," he demanded, "did this conversation get so serious? It's you, Armstrong. This is all your fault. I see I'll have to get you drunk." He picked up the pitcher of beer, started to pour. "Have some more beer, before I start telling you about the trials and tribulations of my kindergarten days."

Even though she accepted the refill, even though she sensed his embarrassment, she wouldn't let him change the subject. "Sorry, Charlie, I heard every word you said, but I still think you're nice. Look at what you did for me with Vince. Look at what you're doing for Fran and Joe right now. If that isn't nice, what is?"

"That's where you're wrong, Armstrong," he drawled.

Unexpectedly, he reached out to cup the edge of her jaw, bringing her closer as he tilted her head to look in her eyes. She didn't, couldn't, pull away.

He stared into that bright, blue-eyed gaze and noted the small stains of color that spotted each cheek. As if of its own volition, his finger lazily traced the fiery trail. "I've never done anything without an ulterior motive in my life."

The electricity, that tiny flare of chemical attraction that had always burned hotly between them, burst into flame, sparking newfound awareness and sensations she'd never experienced before. The pool hall faded into oblivion. Cassie was conscious only of the softness of his touch against her heated skin and those lively gray eyes, strangely tender now.

"You're glinting with rage again," he informed her with a small smile.

"I am not." But she barely breathed the words. She was losing control, had lost control, and like a drowning man going down for the third time, she had to ask the next question. "So what do you get this time, Charlie Whitman?"

He lowered his face so their lips were mere inches apart. So close, his warm breath fanned her cheek. "Close your eyes, Armstrong. I'm going to kiss you."

She knew with some uncanny prescience that once he did, she'd be lost, but she didn't stop him. Somebody else did.

"Hey there, you two," Fran interrupted. "We're ready to go. Now."

As flustered as Charlie and Cassie were, it was impossible to miss Fran's disapproving tone.

"Saved by the bell," Charlie drawled with a sigh, reluctantly releasing Cassie.

"Or the bodyguard," she corrected tightly.

Charlie smiled at her, noting with pleased surprise the irritated frustration in her voice. It precisely matched the way he felt inside right about now, tied up in knots of unfulfilled desire and strangled want. "Something tells me your friend does not approve of me."

That proved an understatement. On the ride home, the strong-willed Fran maneuvered it so that the cab dropped off Joe and Cassie first, leaving her alone with Charlie.

"Good luck," Cassie whispered as Charlie escorted her to her building. "I'd tell Fran to mind her own business, but—" she sighed "—I'm afraid it wouldn't do any good."

"You still owe me a date, Armstrong. You're not planning to welch on me after you've heard about my checkered past, are you?"

She smiled reassuringly. "Not a chance, Whitman. I'm not letting you off the hook that easy."

He wanted to kiss her so badly it scared him a little, but wary of watchful eyes, he contented himself with whispering, "I had fun tonight." It was true, he had. Not the fun and games he usually had on a date, but something beyond that.

"Me, too," Cassie whispered.

Without even being aware of it, he took a step closer. So did she.

"Charlie!" Fran called from within the idling cab.

"Eyes of an eagle," Charlie complained. "To our date," he whispered.

Cassie smiled a little uncertainly now. "I just hope you live long enough to collect."

As all advertising people worth their salt knew, the best defense was a good offense, so once alone with Fran, Charlie decided to take the bull by the horns. An analogy that proved only too accurate. "So, Fran," he said pleasantly, "something on your mind?"

Across the seat and through the darkness, she skewered him with her eyes. "What kind of game are you playing, Charlie Whitman?"

"I'm sure I don't know what you mean, Fran."

"Can it, Whitman. Save the cutesy Peter Pan routine for the nymphets. You're talking to me now."

"You're such a tough cookie." He was trying to control his temper, something rarely aroused, but it was a losing battle.

"You bet, buddy. I grew up in the school of hard knocks, same as you. But Cassie didn't."

"Aha, I was waiting for that name to cross your lips. You're not her keeper, Fran."

"No, but I am her friend. And as her friend I'm telling you to lay off, Whitman. Take your little bag of tricks and find some other playmate, because she's not buying your act. I won't let her."

In his anger, he blurted out the truth—something he rarely did. "I like her, Fran. I know you may find that very hard to believe coming from an insensitive lout such as myself, but I do."

In answer, she gave him a cold, hard, appraising stare. He wasn't sure what she read in his expression, but whatever it was, she backed off a little—something Fran Gorham rarely did. "I just hope you know what you're doing, Charlie Whitman."

So did he. Oh, so did he.

5

SEVERAL DAYS LATER, as the early dusk of winter settled over the Manhattan skyline, Charlie strolled into Cassie's office. Catching her unawares, he had to smile at the look of intense concentration on her face, couldn't resist the urge to lean over her desk to lightly graze a kiss against her check.

Her head snapped up and she fought down the urge to blush at the unexpected caress. "Charlie! Where did you come from?"

"Funny, that's what my parents always ask." He laughed when she did, settling his thigh against the corner of her desk. "And speaking of parents, how was the family reunion?"

Cassie grinned. "Well, Timmy graduated. I think my parents were secretly relieved. It was good fun. Except—" a cloud entered her eyes "—I guess I miss them already."

He couldn't imagine missing his parents. If anything, he went out of his way to avoid them. Not that Charles and Sylvia seemed to be pining away for his company, either. Invitations to the Whitman III household were few and far between, which was easier all the way around. In his family, absence did not make the heart grow fonder. Pushing aside somber thoughts, he regarded her lightly. "Well, maybe I have something that will cheer you up."

"And what's that?" Just the sight of him cheered her up. Dressed in the inevitable ripped blue jeans and scuffed deck shoes, he wore a T-shirt that read *Pourquoi Pas?* in tacky red and green fluorescent colors.

A broad grin flashed across his face. "I have come," he informed her, "to claim my bet. You owe me a date, Armstrong. Tonight. And I'm not taking no for an answer. I thought we could go to the beach."

"Beach? It's February, Whitman. And—" her gaze shot to the window, and she observed the flurries that fell from the leaden gray sky "—it's snowing."

"Precisely." He snagged her wrist. "Cuts way down on the crowds. Not to mention, promotes snuggling. Some of that enforced body contact I've been telling you about."

Cassie laughed. "Sounds like fun. I only wish I could go, but—"

"Armstrong, you don't seem to understand how this game is played. When I ask you out, you're supposed to say yes. And you're supposed to find me irresistible."

The truth was, she did. More and more. "I'm sorry, Charlie, but I have another commitment tonight."

His sigh could have been heard all the way out on Fire Island. Arms crossed, a look of exasperation on his face, he demanded, "So who's my competition this time, Armstrong? Fran? The professor? A family member?"

"Not exactly. Tonight's Tuesday. I teach."

He could not have looked more shocked had she suggested a trip to the moon. "Teach?" This time, *his* gaze traveled to the window. "At night?"

Cassie laughed. "Not children, Charlie. Adults. I teach English as a Second Language at City College."

He whistled. "Well, well, well. You really are a paragon of virtue. What is it you do in your spare time, Armstrong? Work with Mother Teresa? Double as an altar boy?"

"You're teasing me again, Charlie Whitman."

He was, but only because he was so intrigued. He had thought, in all modesty, that at the ripe old age of thirty-six, he had women figured out. But he couldn't quite seem to get an angle on this person named Cassie Armstrong. She was unlike any other woman he'd ever met. She was not a babe, a dish or a doll, not someone he could date and then forget. She was not some self-sufficient, queen-of-the-barbs woman of the nineties like Fran or his mother—although his mother stood in a category all by herself in the sacrificing-tongue department—not the type he could spar with and then move on. And she was certainly not some spinsterish drone like every English teacher he'd ever had, the sort he could readily ignore. Cassie Armstrong was an intriguing mix of all three. She was serious yet fun, tough yet vulnerable, and pretty enough in that Ivory-girl sort of way that made him want to kiss her every time he laid eyes on her. In short, she defied classification, refused to fit a mold. Every time he thought he had her figured out, she did something to surprise him, making him come back for more.

"I don't suppose," she heard herself say, telling herself that it was perfectly acceptable for a woman in this liberated day and age to ask a man out, especially when he'd asked her first, "you'd care to meet me after my class for a drink?"

His pulse quickened and he grinned. "Why, Armstrong, you're not suggesting a date, are you? That's awfully forward of you. And I don't know. I mean, this is all so sudden. I have to tell you, I don't usually go out with women who are a combination of Florence Nightingale, Clara Barton and Joan of Arc all rolled into one."

"Forget it, Whitman," she stormed, grabbing her coat. "Just forget I said anything."

Laughing, he stepped forward to help her with it. "I have an even better idea. Why don't I come along with you to class?"

She stopped moving. "And watch me teach?"

"I wouldn't make you nervous, would I?"

Nervous did not begin to describe it. The mere thought of those lively gray eyes upon her made her heart somersault.

He watched as tension crept into her expression, saw the no form on her lips. "Come on, Armstrong, we can discuss strategy for Majik Toys on the way over."

Tension dissolved into disbelief. "You want to discuss strategy? After hours? Pull the other leg, Whitman. Now I've heard everything."

He wouldn't take no for an answer, managing to twist things around so that she didn't even know what they were arguing about as he hustled her out of the agency. "Armstrong, are you questioning my commitment to this business? Are you suggesting I take it any less seriously than you? That my dedication is any less than yours? That—"

"Okay, okay," Cassie finally agreed. She looked around, surprised to find herself out on the street in front of the subway stop. "Now that you've managed to totally confuse the issue, I suppose I'll have to let you come. At least it will keep you off the streets. And who knows?" She sighed. "You might even learn something."

All his skulduggery proved well worth the effort. Watching Cassie Armstrong teach was pure pleasure.

From his vantage point in the back of the room, he saw her nervousness, caught the small, anxious glances she shot his way, and when he saw her relax he knew she had forgotten all about him. He might have come along on a lark, but amusement quickly faded, to be replaced by respect. He had to admit, he was impressed.

She had eighteen students. For the most part, they were older adults who seemed as serious about learning as Cassie was about teaching them. She made it fun, though, and encouraged them to speak out.

"Okay, Mr. Nguyen," Cassie said, addressing an elderly Vietnamese gentleman in a loud Hawaiian-print shirt. "Now suppose someone said to you, 'How are you today?' How would you answer them?"

"I say..." The older man struggled with the unfamiliar tongue. "Okeydokey."

"Very good." Although she didn't like to play favorites, he was her star pupil. "Now you ask me the same question."

His alert dark eyes lit up. "I say, 'How it hangin', baby?'" As the class erupted into laughter, he confessed, "I got from movie. It wrong."

"No, no," Cassie assured him, biting her cheek to keep from laughing. "It's perfect, Mr. Nguyen. I think you've learned everything I know about English. In fact—" she pretended to hand the chalk over to him "—I think you could probably teach me a thing or two."

As the class dissolved into giggles and guffaws, Charlie smiled from the back of the room. Another Cassie Armstrong to add to his collection. This was a different woman from the one he saw at the agency or observed in client presentations. In the classroom, she came alive, her smile ready, her eyes bright. She was in her element.

"You're a good teacher, Armstrong," he told her on the subway ride home. "In fact, you're a great teacher." There was no teasing in his voice.

He expected her to make some self-deprecating remark, but instead she met his gaze straight on. "I know. I love teaching. And the truth is, those people really give me more than I give them. It's so different from advertising. I mean, it's so important, so meaningful."

His gray eyes widened. "You're not suggesting that advertising is a less-than-meaningful profession, are you?"

"Well, it ain't brain surgery," she shot back.

"So, why don't you teach full-time, then?"

A wistful smile formed on her face. "Maybe I will someday. When I pay off all my student loans. Teaching may be rewarding, but it's not exactly profitable. Besides, I'd need to go back for my Ph.D., and I'm tired of the hallowed halls of academia right now. I'd like to experience life a little first."

He toyed with a lock of her hair. "Oh, yeah. Funny, but I happen to know just the guy who can help you."

"I'll bet you do."

When the subway screeched to a halt, they exited into the cold, brisk February night. Like everything else in this fast-moving city, not even snow stuck around. The sidewalk was clear and still crowded with people at nine-thirty at night. As they strolled down Fifty-seventh Street he reached for her hand, companionably swinging their entwined grip between them. Like an old married couple, Cassie thought. She had only known this man two months, yet it seemed much longer. She had never felt this close to any man. Not Jeff. Not even her lover in college. Charlie Whitman was different, special. She felt comfortable with him, although comfortable was an odd word to use for a man who could turn her knees to jelly with a grin. But then, that was part of Charlie's charm and allure. She could never be entirely sure what he would do, how he would react. The combination of comfort and exhilaration was a powerful one.

Waiting to cross the street, she tilted her head to study him. "So, how come *you* do it, Charlie? How come you work in advertising?"

Beneath his worn leather jacket, he pointed to his T-shirt. *"Pourquoi pas?"* he asked.

"Ah, yes, the infamous Charlie Whitman philosophy of life. Why not? The answer to everything."

Stopping in front of her building, he rested his hands on her shoulders, smiling into her eyes. In that moment, her cheeks bright red with cold, she looked about ten years old and so appealing he almost kissed her. "And do you have a better one?"

Once upon a time, not too long ago, she might have argued with him, but the truth was she was beginning to suspect he was right. Sometimes in life, you just had to jump in with both feet and take your chances. Which was exactly what she planned to do right now. "Would you care to come in for that drink I promised you?"

"Sure." As they waited for the elevator, he studied her. She was different tonight, more relaxed, more confident, almost as if she'd made a decision about something . . . or someone.

Leaning negligently against the wall, he smiled at the complicated series of locks on her door, grinned when she fumbled with them. "Take your time, Armstrong. I've got all night."

Concentrating on the locks, she tried to ignore that bright-eyed glance. "You can't be too careful, you know."

"Oh, I know. Any riffraff could walk in off the street. Look at me."

She was trying not to. "Teasing, Whitman," she warned. "You're teasing me again."

"I thought you'd be used to it by now."

Smiling, she met his eye. "I guess I am."

At last, the multiple locks yielded. "Make yourself at home," she invited, then caught herself. Charlie was already restlessly wandering the room. For a moment, she'd forgotten who she was talking to. Charlie Whitman never stood on ceremony.

Her apartment looked exactly the way he'd expected. Like Cassie Armstrong herself, it was neat, very neat, but somehow it was homey and comfortable, too. Unlike his parents' mausoleum, it looked like somebody's home, not just a showplace for possessions. There was a bright throw on the sofa, there were potted plants by the window, and from atop an old, badly scratched piano, Armstrong family photographs smiled at him. Though he told himself he wasn't checking, he noted there was no evidence of male habitation, not even a picture.

Surprised she was not more nervous, she hung their coats neatly in the closet. Even his jacket made her smile. The leather was well-worn, almost rubbed thin in places. On Charlie Whitman's salary he could have easily afforded a new one, several new ones. But then, unlike most other people who worked in the advertising business, Charlie obviously wasn't into things. It was just one of the many things she liked about him. "What would you like to drink, Charlie? I have some beer or wine, domestic, I'm afraid. And sorry, but there's no hard liquor. I'm not much of a drinker, to tell you the truth."

"Beer's fine," he answered absently, squatting in front of her bookcase. He'd often thought people's choice of reading material told a lot about them. Cassie's selection was as complex as the woman herself. Serious tomes competed with popular bestsellers, and he even uncovered a romance or two. All looked well thumbed and well enjoyed, a far cry from his parents' extensive library. They collected first editions; reading them would have been beside the point.

One title in particular leaped off the shelf. Frost's *Anthology.* He thumbed to a page, but quoted the first and last stanza of "The Road Not Taken" from memory.

Across the length of the room, their eyes met. He caught the surprise in hers. "Well, don't look so shocked, Armstrong. I do manage to use my head for more than a hat rack once in a while. Something had to rub off from those five prep schools I attended, if only by osmosis."

"It's not that." She knew Charlie was bright, very bright—in fact, probably smarter than she. Nobody possessed Charlie's command of the English language. "It's just, well . . . that's my favorite poem."

"Mine, too. Small world, huh? Maybe we do have something in common, after all."

She thought they did. Maybe more than a little. But not wanting to give herself away, she teased him instead. "You and I? What do we have in common, Whitman, other than liking the same poem?"

"We both like beer," he pointed out. "And speaking of which, I'm thirsty."

With a laugh, she headed into the kitchen and he trailed after her. "Everything in its place and a place for everything," he observed, shaking his head at the spotless countertops. "Sorry, Armstrong, but that's not something we have in common."

"I know. I've been in your office, remember."

He scoffed at that. "You think that's bad, you should see my apartment."

Her movements slowed. "I'd like to."

He stopped roaming long enough to smile at her. "Do you realize, Armstrong, this is the first time we've ever been alone together? I mean, really alone."

Bending over in front of the refrigerator, she extracted two bottles, then straightened to look at him. "I know," she answered softly. She found a bottle opener in a drawer then proceeded to calmly pop off the tops.

Watching her, he had to ask the next question. "Do I make you nervous?"

Half turning, she squarely met him in the eye. "No."

"God, I must be slipping."

His answer was so predictably Charlie that Cassie had to laugh, and at the sound he came up behind her. Sliding his hands around her waist, he pulled her against him. As he rested his chin against the bright fall of her hair, he breathed in the pure, clean scent of honeysuckle. "Fran's not going to save you this time, Armstrong," he whispered in her ear.

"I don't think I want to be saved."

As if by magic, she turned in his arms to face him. He didn't need any further invitation.

The instant his lips closed in on hers, she was lost. All reserve, all the reasons she should not like this man vanished into thin air as pure instinct took over. For once in her sane, ordered existence, Cassie Armstrong listened to the urgings of her heart and not the logic of her mind.

She would have expected impatience from this man, but Charlie took his time. Nibbling at her lips, he ran his fingers through her thick mane of hair until Cassie thought she might die of want.

It was she who quickened the pace, she who opened her mouth against the onslaught of his. She moaned low in her throat when his tongue mated boldly with hers. His grip tightened almost painfully in her hair as the kiss went on and on.

It was Charlie who finally ended it. Breathing hard, he pulled back to stare down into those luminous blue eyes. He smiled. "Well, that was certainly worth the wait."

She was gratified to read surprise in his expression. She might not be the voice of experience in matters of the flesh, but she trusted her instincts and she possessed enough self-confidence and self-awareness to know what was right for her. Instinct told her this man was right. He might not have been the man she would have imagined for herself, but he was right.

She didn't love Charlie Whitman. She didn't believe in love at first sight. Love was something that had to be nurtured and grow if it was to stand the test of time; she'd learned that from her parents. And she was not naive enough to believe he loved her. But she knew, where it counted, that she could grow to love him. The thought made her smile.

Cassie was right about Charlie Whitman being surprised . . . and shaken, not only at the depth of her passion, but at the strength of his. She was vulnerable yet powerful, and this strange contradiction evoked a complicated reaction within him. He wanted to ravish her, and at the same time he felt strangely tender toward her, almost protective.

He did not love her. But he thought he could. And the thought terrified him.

This was not supposed to happen. Charlie Whitman did not like complications. He had survived his thirty-six years on earth by being fast of foot and fleet of mouth. His childhood with Charles and Sylvia had taught him one invaluable lesson—love hurts. As a child he couldn't help but love his parents. It was an automatic response, like waking up in the morning or breathing. But no matter how hard he tried, no matter how much he'd turned and twisted himself inside out to please them, he'd known by the age of eight that they would never love him back. Over the years and through the pain, he'd added a parable of his own—hurt first or be hurt. He had never been in love, and never planned to be in love. Nobody was ever going to get that close again.

The thought that she was an entirely different person than his parents never crossed his mind. He was consumed with one thought and one thought only—*escape.*

Immediately he withdrew to a safe corner of the kitchen and stuffed his hands into the pockets of his disreputable jeans. He looked everywhere but directly at her as he muttered under his breath. "Well, I gotta go."

He did not have to see her expression to read her surprise.

"But it's so early, and you haven't even had your beer yet."

"I don't feel too good," he mumbled, retreating toward the front door. That, at least, was the truth. He did feel ill. His stomach churned, his knees felt weak, and claustrophobia threatened to overtake him at any second.

Cassie might have protested further, but he didn't give her the chance. Besides he did look sick, she thought, as she handed him his coat. Pale and shaken. "I hope you feel better."

"Oh, it'll pass." And the funny thing was, it did. The minute he was alone on the street.

IN THE DAYS that followed, he managed to do a little better around her. He was witty, teasing, the perfect Charlie Whitman of their prekiss days. But he treated her like a big brother and in no way, shape, manner or form did he allude to the kiss they'd shared on that snowy winter's eve. Had she not caught him eyeing her several times when he thought she wasn't looking, she might have thought she'd imagined the whole thing. But his strangely haunted gaze convinced her that she had not made anything up.

At first, his bizarre reaction puzzled her. She replayed their final scene in her mind a thousand times, trying to figure out if something she'd said or done might have offended him. Each time, she came up empty, until finally, when she could stand it no more, she confronted him. Not being a woman given to game-playing or artifice she met the dilemma head-on.

"Is something wrong, Charlie?" she asked, cornering him alone in his office.

Damn, he thought, but his smile was bright and quick. "Wrong? Why, whatever could be wrong? You're wearing that worried frown again, Armstrong. Didn't your mother ever warn you that your face might stay that way?"

This time, she wouldn't play. "I think we should talk, Charlie. How about tonight?"

He hesitated only a beat. "Sure, sure, a bunch of us are heading over to Cronin's. Why don't you come along? It'll be fun."

That was not exactly what she had in mind, so she begged off.

But puzzled surprise quickly turned to hurt and finally anger in Cassie's heart.

She avoided Fran whenever possible, dreading that sorrowful I-told-you-so expression on her friend's face. Besides, it was hard to be around a couple in love the way Fran and Joe clearly were these days. But even without discussing it, she could just hear Fran say,

"Honey, what did I tell you? With Charlie Whitman it's the thrill of the chase and once that's gone, poof, so is he."

Except Cassie Armstrong was a perceptive woman, and she knew Charlie's problem went deeper than that. She knew what they'd shared had been special, and that Charlie had thought so, too. From the sidelines, she quietly watched Charlie laugh and flirt. *Coward,* she thought. *Charlie Whitman, you are a coward.*

Life went on even without Charlie Whitman. Cassie managed to get some work done, and she went out with Jeff Paulson a few times. But she supposed that, along with the hurt, Charlie had taught her something, too, something valuable about herself. Though she liked Jeff, she knew she would never love him. On the surface, the good professor was perfect for her, but Jeff Paulson didn't make her smile at the mere sight of him, and try though he might, he couldn't make her laugh.

CHARLIE WHITMAN was not doing much laughing these days. He told himself he should be deliriously happy. He was, after all, a free man. That was what he'd wanted. But sometimes in life the worst thing that can happen is that you get what you want, or at least what you think you want, and that was exactly what happened to Charlie Whitman. Somehow his precious freedom lost much of its allure as the days slid into weeks. He tried the conventional panaceas of wine, women and song, but only found himself nursing a hangover and bored out of his skull. The redhead he'd once thought so luscious had the body of a Miss America but possessed the brains of a ditz. A classically beautiful blonde now left him cold. None of them was Cassie Armstrong, which should have been good, but somehow it was bad. Beneath the laughing face of the clown, he was lonely, scared and confused.

He turned to writing. He had always kept a diary, ever since he was a child. Words were his salvation and his sanity, helping him sort out his world. And without consciously deciding to do so, he began a novel. The title came easily. *Commitments*, he typed into his ancient and trusty Royal. Somehow the chapters flowed one into the other, until one day, hunched in his chair, the answer came to him clear as a bell.

"Damn," he muttered. He missed Cassie Armstrong, and he wanted her back in his life. It was as simple and as complicated as that. Now all he had to do was convince her to give him a second chance.

Finding a time to promote his cause proved more difficult than he'd imagined, compounded by the fact that he lost his nerve on more than one occasion and that Cassie avoided him like the plague.

Finally, one night, opportunity presented itself. Across the length of the agency lobby he spotted her, and for once she was alone. Though the setting was less than romantic, beggars couldn't be choosers, and Charlie planned to beg.

Halfway across the lobby, he stopped dead in his tracks. It was not cowardice that stopped him, but the arrival of a man—one she was clearly expecting, from the smile on her face. With his lanky blond hair and aviator frames, the newcomer looked tweedy and civilized. *The professor*, Charlie assumed. He was too late.

A dull heaviness in his heart, he watched them smile at one another. Like Ken and Barbie, they were perfectly matched, perfectly suited. He told himself it was just as well. At least she was happy. He took some small consolation in that as he turned away.

6

WHEN VINCE DEMANDED a meeting with all the top-level agency brass who worked on his toy lines, the request caught Cassie off guard. Particularly when Vince, in his usually tight-lipped fashion, refused to divulge the meeting's agenda. Knowing her client the way she did, and given his history, or nonhistory, with agencies, she suspected the news would not be good. Still, she tried not to think the worst. The account was going fairly well, she reminded herself, with no real dissension between them. If anything, she seemed to have gained Vince's grudging respect, and the agency product had improved because of it. But as the agency personnel filed past her into the mahogany-paneled conference room, Cassie's stomach churned. Her tension only multiplied when Charlie Whitman finagled it so that he and Cassie were the last to enter the room. Bad news must come in threes.

They had never really talked since that fateful snowy night almost a month ago, and she had no intention of speaking to him now. As she always did these days, she tried to sidle past him, but he was a man determined.

Blocking her path, he forced the issue. "So how are you, Cassie?"

"Fine," she lied, avoiding his eyes. She refused to ask how he was. She told herself she didn't care.

He was grateful she didn't. The truth was, he was miserable.

"If you'll excuse me," she managed stiffly. "I think the meeting's about to start."

But he wouldn't let her go. She always had some excuse these days. Snatched opportunities were the only times he was alone with her anymore, and he made the most of this one. Glancing around to make sure no one was listening, he lowered his tone. "I'd like to talk to you sometime."

Not now, Charlie, she thought. *Please, not now.* Deliberately, she chose to misunderstand him, and even more deliberately she kept her voice pleasant and businesslike. "Fine. Make an appointment with my secretary. I'm sure she can fit you in. But as you can see, I'm a little busy right now, so if you don't mind . . ."

She tried to shoulder past him, but he gripped her arm, preventing escape. At his touch, Cassie jerked.

Charlie sighed. Her reaction only underscored his point. "We need to talk, Cassie. Soon. Please."

The *please* almost undid her. Almost, but not quite. She hung on to indifference; it was safer that way. "I told you, make an appointment."

He wasn't willing to back down, either. "This isn't exactly business, Armstrong."

"Then I fail to see what we have to talk about."

"How about what happened?"

For the first time, she met his gaze. "Nothing happened, Charlie. Absolutely nothing. Now I have a meeting to attend, and so do you."

This time, he made no move to stop her as she strode past him into the conference room. What was the use? She wouldn't listen.

Still, as the meeting convened, hope sprang eternal. Some masochistic tendency made him select the seat next to hers at the conference table. He tried not to notice when she stiffened and moved fractionally away.

THE SMALL EXCHANGE summed up the relationship between Cassie Armstrong and Charlie Whitman these days. That is, there was no relationship.

Cassie maintained a strict demeanor of polite indifference. After all, if nothing else, she had her pride. She tried to keep their exchanges businesslike and to a minimum and always when they were surrounded by other people. Mostly because she did not trust herself otherwise. For right beneath the surface, anger and hurt bubbled like a smoldering volcano, threatening to blow at the slightest provocation. And the fact that she had only herself to blame for the situation made her angrier still. The only thing Charlie Whitman was guilty of was kissing her once—hardly the stuff of shotgun weddings. He certainly had never promised her a thing. If anything, he had warned her off. Everyone had warned her off. No, that she'd gotten hurt was entirely her own fault, and she was better off out of the relationship, if one could even call it that. All the common sense and logic, however, couldn't change the immutable fact that what she felt toward this man was anything but polite indifference. The truth was, she alternated between wanting to rip his lungs out and wanting to shake him until his teeth rattled in his head while asking him why he'd been such a fool. Not exactly an ideal state of affairs to maintain with a colleague, but there it was.

Charlie saw only the politely indifferent facade. He wanted to explain what had happened to him. He wanted to beg her forgiveness. Most of all, he wanted to ask her if she was happy with Jeff Paulson. But he never got the chance. Whenever he got close to her, which admittedly was not often, she froze him out, looked past him. They couldn't go on like this. At least he couldn't. He had to find a way to make her listen. But when? How? That's what he couldn't seem to figure out.

THE MEETING BEGAN with a bang.

"You're fired," Vince announced to the assembled troops of Woodson & Meyers Advertising, Inc. The client was dressed in his customary thousand-dollar suit, but he possessed all the subtlety of a panzer division as he landed the death knell. "I'm firing the agency as of today."

It was an agency person's worst nightmare. The Damocles' sword under which they lived, but never really got used to. Here today, gone tomorrow. The price paid for living life in the fast lane.

As articulate as the assembled group was, shocked surprise held them silent. It wasn't as if ol' Vince hadn't done this countless times, yet there had been no hints, no clues as to what he had in store for them. As the news penetrated, the agency staff shared wide-eyed glances around the table, most of them settling in Cassie's direction. She was the senior-ranking account person in the room, so the mantle of responsibility fell heavily on her shoulders, a burden no one envied as she took the lead.

The fact that she was no less shocked than the others did not bode well for the group. "What?" she gasped. "You can't do this! We have a contract."

Wrong tack. Vince's powerful beady eyes switched to high beam, zeroing in on her like a hunter sighting prey. "I'm breakin' it. I got my own lawyers, not that I trust those mealymouthed bastards, either. But one thing I know, I don't gotta do nothing but die or pay taxes."

There was a certain irrefutable logic to that. And of course, if their client was an expert at anything, it was firing ad agencies. So much for the legal approach, Cassie thought, abandoning that in favor of dollar-and-cents practicality. "But you'll lose money on your media buys if you let us go now. We've already committed to the spots, and they'll charge you anyway. Look, I'm sure if you just give us time, we can work this out."

But Vince was already shrugging his custom-built shoulders. "So, I'll lose money. So big deal. It'll be worth it. I want you out."

"But why?" she pleaded, not just for herself but for all the jobs around the table. There was no telling what might happen if they lost this account. "I'm sorry if we've done anything wrong, anything that displeases you. If you're not satisfied, surely if we put our heads together we can solve the problem. Now, if you could just tell me what the problem is . . ."

Vince Bertolli had not clawed and scratched his way to the top of his dog-eat-dog world by being moved by pretty speeches. "No reason," he stated flatly. "I just want you out. That's all. Now."

"But that doesn't make any sense," Cassie persisted, determined not to go down without a fight. But she was tilting at windmills. A client did not have to make sense, that was the problem. The agency was subject to his whims and foibles, as every person around the room knew all too well.

Seated next to Cassie, Charlie Whitman decided he'd heard just about enough. Logic and sentiment were not getting them anywhere. Drastic action was called for. Being a gambler at heart, and knowing Vince the way he did, he took a big risk. "Well, I think he's right," Charlie declared loudly. "In fact, I'll go one step further. I think we deserve to be fired."

Everyone in the room stared at Charlie in open-mouthed stupefaction. But Charlie saw he had Vince's attention, and there was slight confusion in those beady eyes, which was exactly what Charlie wanted. Beside him, Cassie glared. "What do you think you're doing, Whitman?" she said through her teeth. "Just shut up. Now."

"Play along," Charlie told her under his breath. "Yes," he said aloud. "In fact, Cassie and I were just discussing the problem with this account's advertising the other day. And do you know what we said?"

No, nobody could even begin to guess what had been said, least of all Cassie herself.

Charlie answered for them. "Synergy," he said succinctly. "There's no synergy between this account's advertising. No broad strategy that covers all the product lines. That's not good advertising. In fact, it almost looks like someone picked the copy, eenie, meenie, minie, moe." Which, of course, was exactly what happened. He glanced at Cassie. "Isn't that right, Cassie? Isn't that what we said?"

She risked a glance at Vince, saw him nodding slightly. You are one lucky SOB, Charlie Whitman, she thought, knowing now exactly what he was up to. "Well, yes," she agreed. "Not in those exact words, of course, but yes, that was the general gist of our conversation."

Charlie turned to Vince. "I'm sure this goes along with some of your own thinking on this."

Vince nodded slowly. "Yeah, you know it's not like I really wanted to fire you guys. Hey, I like you all. And I like our advertising. Hell, I picked it. But some of the boys have been talkin'. And that's what they're tellin' me. That my spots have no—" He glanced at Charlie. "What'd you call it?"

"Synergy," Charlie supplied for him.

"Yeah, yeah, that's it. Synergy."

So that was what this whole thing was about. Loss of face. Vince Bertolli wasn't smart enough to know good advertising when he saw it, but he had people working for him who did. And as usual, instead of Vince taking the rap for what he'd done and admitting he'd been wrong, he'd conveniently blamed it on the agency. The standard advertising catch-22. Please the client, lose the account. It was just what Charlie'd warned Cassie about that day so long ago, before their first Majik Toy presentation.

She, too, remembered that day. She spoke up. "Which is why we'd like to design a new umbrella campaign for you, Mr. Bertolli. An umbrella campaign that will encompass all your product lines under one strategy. If you'll give us a month, I'm sure we can come up with something you can be proud of."

Vince leaned back in his chair, his paunch straining the buttons of his custom-made shirt. "Hey, I'm a reasonable man but . . ."

"Two weeks," Charlie jumped in. "Just two weeks."

"One week," Vince told them. "Seven days from today. Or else." His voice brooked no argument. The godfather had made them an offer they couldn't refuse.

OUTSIDE the Majik Toy building, the agency staff convened in private. "One week," Cassie sighed, rubbing her forehead tiredly. She felt as if they'd won the battle but lost the war. "How are we going to come up with a brand-new campaign in seven days?"

"Off campus," Charlie told them, trying to sound confident. "All of us go someplace together for seven days and six nights and we do nothing but eat, sleep and drink Majik Toys."

Dismal silence fell over the group. Being the consummate professionals they were, they knew they had no choice, and no one complained, but privately each was consumed with his or her own personal dilemma at this unanticipated interruption in their lives.

There goes my chance to finally see the Rolling Stones, thought Scott Findell, the twenty-three-year-old account executive. *So much for those impossible-to-come-by Madison Square Garden tickets.*

Oh, my God! Tom Garnett, the research director, was in a panic. *My wife is due any day now. How can I disappear for seven days?*

A week without Fran, Joe thought. *Why, we haven't been apart since that night in the pool hall.*

None of their misgivings compared to the fear and panic in Cassie Armstrong's heart. She might not have concert tickets, a pregnant spouse or a loved one to leave behind, but in her opinion she had an even more insurmountable problem. How in the world was she going to remain politely indifferent to Charlie Whitman when she'd be living on top of him for a week?

Only Charlie Whitman smiled. He hadn't exactly planned on this turn of events. But it was, as they said, an unexpected windfall. Not even Cassie Armstrong could avoid him now.

IN A SECLUDED HOTEL, an hour away from the city, the group met that evening, luggage in hand. The lush, fertile greenness of Westchester County's Hudson Valley was wasted on the agency staff. Around the conference table, blank paper and freshly sharpened pencils in hand, they regarded each other glumly.

Two hours later, when they agreed to disband for the night, the pads remained pristinely fresh and their pencils sharpened to a fare-thee-well. As for Charlie, unless "Pass the beer nuts" signified a softening in Cassie's attitude, he was not doing any better in the romance department than he was on the account. But at least she had spoken to him. That in itself was a departure from the norm, and he chose to take it as a positive sign, which proved how truly desperate he was these days.

A good part of the creative block, he knew, was the tension between Cassie and himself. He intended to rectify that as soon as he could get her alone.

"Well, that was certainly enlightening," Charlie said as they yawned their way out of the room. "Anyone for a nightcap?"

"I gotta call my wife."

The research guy dashed for his room, Joe hot on his heels. "I gotta call Fran," he muttered over his shoulder.

Perfect, Charlie thought. "Cassie?"

Her face froze into its usual pleasant lines. "Sorry, I'm too tired." Preferring to stick with the safety of Joe and the others, she hurried after them toward the elevator.

Scott, the account guy, said, "I could use a beer."

"Forget it," Charlie snapped. "You're too young to drink. And isn't it past your bedtime, anyway?" Leaving the openmouthed account executive, he hightailed it after the young man's boss, catching up to the group as the elevator doors slid open.

Cassie looked past him, but Joe took note of his entrance. In typical Joe fashion, he missed the entire point behind the exercise. "I thought you were having a drink?"

"Changed my mind," Charlie told him shortly, hoping he'd catch on.

Of course Joe didn't. As the elevator doors slid open at the third floor, the art director waited for his roommate, a puzzled look on his face when Charlie made no move to get off the elevator.

"Hey, Charlie, this is our floor," Joe told him, holding open the doors.

"Thanks anyway, Joe, but you go ahead. I think I'll explore a little." At the confused expression on Joe's face, Charlie sighed then jerked his head toward Cassie.

As realization finally dawned, Joe suddenly let out an "Oh!" of comprehension, then grinned. "Good luck." Cassie would have been an idiot to miss it.

Alone at last, Charlie thought. "What can I tell you?" he joked, trying to cover up Joe's faux pas. "True love. It addles the mind."

Cassie ignored him. She really wouldn't know about true love, now would she?

In the face of her silence, he tried again. "You don't mind if I ride with you, do you?"

She did, but what could she say? Staring at the elevator numbers, she shrugged. "It's a free country."

So it was. He opted for another ice-breaking opening. "So how do you think the session went?"

"Slow." A lot like this ride. The elevator crawled past four, inching toward her room on eight.

So much for icebreakers. Knowing he might never get another opportunity, Charlie plunged right in. "Look, Cassie," he said, wanting no artifice between them now. "I'm sorry things turned out so badly. And I know it's no excuse, but all I can say is, I got scared. I know I was wrong and I'm sorry if I hurt you but I just got panicky."

There. He'd said it. Perhaps not well, but at least he'd finally said it.

He stole a look at Cassie, trying to read her face, but as usual lately her expression gave nothing away. They might have been discussing the weather for all the emotion in her eyes. She looked particularly pretty tonight, and the thought of all he'd had, and all he'd thrown away, made him almost physically ill.

He didn't know what it cost her to keep her face an impassive mask. Didn't know how hard it was for her to say lightly, "Well, good thing it didn't go any further, huh, Charlie? We shared a few laughs, right? Well, live and learn."

When the elevator doors sprang open, she was out of that small cubicle like a shot. She hadn't, however, counted on Charlie Whitman's persistence. Determined to have this out, he doggedly tagged after her.

When she stopped in front of her room, so did he. "Charlie, you're forgiven, okay?" Her hand shook as she fumbled in her bag for the magnetic room key.

Charlie was having his own problems. For once in his life, he couldn't find the words to express what he wanted to say. "Cassie, I just want you to be happy, okay?" He addressed the back of her head. "And if the professor makes you happy. . ." His voice trailed off.

This wasn't about Jeff Paulson, Cassie reminded herself. This was about Charlie Whitman. He wanted out, but he didn't want to feel guilty about her. Well, fine. She would make it easy for him, easy for both of them. "Of course, I'm happy, Charlie. Why wouldn't I be happy?"

It was an award-winning performance. But she refused to face him, afraid of the pure misery he'd read in her eyes.

He hadn't realized he was holding his breath until it escaped in one long whoosh. Well, what had he expected? That she would fall into his arms, all forgiven? He thought about pursuing his cause, but there was no point. She was happy with this other guy. She had said so herself. It was over, done, finished. Let it be.

His shoulders slumped wearily, but Cassie didn't see that. All she heard were his next words.

"Well. I'm just glad you're happy. Maybe we could be—" he almost cringed "—friends."

It cut like a knife to her heart. "Sure," she managed. Throat tight with unshed tears, she pushed against the door. "Now, if you'll excuse me, I have a call to make."

Of course, Charlie thought, the professor, and he slunk off to his room.

THEIR HEART-TO-HEART, intended to make things better, only made things worse. They didn't even have false hope to cling to anymore. As the days dragged on, few creative sparks lit the assembled cast, who were all brought down by Charlie's and Cassie's morose expressions. By the end of the fifth day, the entire group was sick of them.

That night as Charlie stared at the ceiling of their hotel room for the fifth evening in a row, Joe sighed loudly.

"They broke up," he announced with typical succinctness.

The news failed to penetrate Charlie's stupor.

"I said!" Joe spoke louder. "They broke up."

Arms behind his head, Charlie looked from the ceiling to his friend. "What?"

In exasperation, Joe practically shouted at him. "They broke up. Cassie and Jeff broke up."

Charlie struggled to sit up. "When?"

Joe shrugged. "Couple of weeks ago."

"Why didn't you tell me?"

"Fran."

Now that made sense. What didn't was . . . Charlie stopped midthought. Now why hadn't Cassie told him that? Unless . . . Could it be? He was out of bed in a flash, tugging on his jeans and T-shirt. He was halfway out the door before Joe stopped him.

"Where you goin'?"

"To see Cassie," Charlie announced impatiently, thrusting his bare feet into his beat-up boat shoes.

"But it's midnight."

"I know." For the first time in days, Charlie grinned. "It's perfect. Catch her with her guard down."

He was right about that. When a knock sounded on her door, the last person on earth she expected to see through her peephole was Charlie Whitman. He'd been avoiding her as assiduously as she'd avoided him for the last few days. "Whitman, what do you want? Do you know what time it is?"

"Yeah, midnight. Now open up. I need to talk to you."

"We've already talked." What was this? Some new form of torture? Were they going to rehash how he was too afraid to get involved? "Go away."

"Cassie, open up. This is important." He hammered against the door so loudly Cassie feared he'd wake her neighbors. "Stop it," she yelled. "You're going to wake up the entire hotel."

"Probably," he responded, still pounding. "But I'm not leaving until you open this door."

"All right. All right. Wait a minute." Clad in only a thin shortie nightgown, the lightest to pack, she fumbled in the hall closet for a robe that was not much better. Instead of opening the door, she compromised by sliding it open a discreet crack. "Now what is so all-fired important that you had to wake me up in the middle of the night?"

Actually, she had not been sleeping, but staring at the ceiling, counting the tiles, a newfound occupation that consumed most of her sleepless nights.

Backlit by the harsh fluorescent hallway light, he peered at her through the crack. "Armstrong," he sighed. "Would you please open this door?"

"First tell me what you want."

He dragged a hand through his curly hair. "It's personal."

Balefully, she met his gaze.

"Okay, fine," he said. "You want to have a highly personal conversation in the middle of a hallway, hey, that's your business. You're always the one who's so concerned about what people think." He paused, but the door didn't open. "Why didn't you tell me you and that guy broke up?"

Whatever she'd expected Charlie Whitman to say, it was not that. She stared at him. "That's what you had to ask me in the middle of the night?"

Seeing he'd made her nervous, Charlie knew he was on the right track. "Why?"

She bit her lip. "Charlie, I really don't see that it's any of your business, and I'm not going to have this conversation in the middle of a hallway so—"

"Good. Then let me in."

Tension combined with sleeplessness erupted into violence, and she attempted to slam the door. "No way."

Too late she realized Charlie had inserted a size-twelve moccasin into the crack.

"Ow!" he cried.

"Good." She leaned against the door with all her weight. "I hope it's broken. It serves you right."

He wasn't giving up. Despite the pain, he pushed with such force that the chain groaned, threatening to give. "We're having this conversation one way or the other, Armstrong," he said through gritted teeth. "Now open up."

She heard the steely determination in his voice, knew he was right. They had to talk, if only for the sake of the account. When she undid the chain, Charlie all but fell into the room.

Retreating a safe distance, she regarded him coolly. "All right, you're in. Now what?" Arms crossed, she stared at him, her eyes holding a challenge and a dare.

But Charlie wasn't looking at her eyes. Even as he regained his balance, he felt himself lose it again. The sight of her in that shortie robe, her long winter white legs bare and silky, made his mouth go dry and all good intentions flee his mind. He dragged his gaze to her face and almost backed down again at the frozen icicles in her expression. An angry Cassie Armstrong was a formidable sight, but he made himself go on. "Why didn't you tell me you broke up with him, Cassie?"

"It's none of your damned business," she snapped.

In a single stride, he crossed the room and grabbed her arm. "I'm making it my business."

She jerked her elbow away. She glared at him, too angry to pull her punches now. "Why?" she demanded. "What difference does it make? You wanted out, so now you're out. Disappear, fly away, take off. That's what you do best anyway. So go ahead. There's the door. Go."

He stood his ground. "Not this time. I want another chance, Cassie. That's what I was trying to tell you when you misled me about the professor."

Afraid to believe, afraid to hope, she felt a measure of anger leaving her, only to be replaced by wariness. "Who told you, anyway?"

"Sorry, but I can't divulge my sources."

"Joe. That little snitch."

Charlie shook his head. "Very loyal friend. He saw how miserable I was without you and—" He took a deep breath, then took an even bigger gamble than he had with Vince. "How miserable you were without me."

That got her back up. "I am not miserable, Charlie Whitman. In fact, I wouldn't go out with you again if you were the last man left on the face of this earth. I am over you."

"Then why," he asked calmly, "are you so angry?"

"I am not angry." She glared at him. "I am indifferent. Absolutely, sublimely indifferent."

He laughed. "You're no more indifferent to me than I am to you. Face it, Armstrong. You're so angry right now, you could take my head off." And you know something? I don't blame you. I deserve it. So go ahead. I'll give you one free shot." He patted his cheek.

She stared at him. "You're not suggesting that I hit you, are you? Because that's crazy, ridiculous and totally juvenile."

"Yep. But it'll make you feel better, so let me have it."

She chose instead to fight with words. "You know what you are, Charlie Whitman? You are a fool, a jerk and a coward."

"All true." He patted his cheek. "So go ahead, take your best shot."

The fact that he'd agreed with her only made her angrier. Her hand curled into a fist. "You know, I should take you up on that offer."

"Go ahead," he invited. "You're not chicken, Armstrong, are you?"

It was like waving a flag in front of a bull. Cassie saw red. "You've got some nerve saying that to me, Whitman."

When it came right down to it, he never thought she'd go through with it. Once again, he'd underestimated Cassie Armstrong.

With a muffled oath, she attacked. The next thing he knew, an uppercut worthy of Jack Dempsey in his prime unfailingly connected with his eye. In one bone-crunching instant, the tables turned. It was Charlie who saw red, not to mention stars.

Her rage subsided as quickly as it had come. Stung by remorse, she stepped back, horrified at what she'd done, at what he'd driven her to do. She was not a violent person, had not thought herself capable of such an act. But Charlie Whitman aroused powerful emotions within her. She was only beginning to figure that out. "Oh, my God, Charlie," she breathed. "I think I just gave you a black eye."

Gingerly, he dabbed the wounded area. "It certainly feels that way." He pulled his hand down. "How does it look?"

Wincing, she looked away. "You don't want to know. Let me get you some ice, or a cold cloth or something." He waved her ministrations aside, and too exhausted to fight with him anymore, she flopped down on the bed and hung her head in her hands. "Charlie Whitman, what am I going to do with you?"

"Give me another chance." Though he joined her on the bed, he didn't touch her. He was wise enough to know this had to be her choice, with no persuasion from him, as persuasive as he could be.

She snuck a sideways look at him. "You mean you still want to?"

For emphasis he enunciated every word. "Cassie Armstrong, go out with me."

She sighed. "The only problem is, Charlie, you say that to all the girls."

"Naw." He grinned, or at least he tried to. "Only the ones who can beat me up." He winced, touching his eye. "Just don't make me laugh, okay? It hurts too much."

The hilarity of the situation struck them both. As Cassie's giggles dissolved into outright laughter, Charlie joined in as best he could, all the while holding his eye.

A pounding on the adjoining wall sobered them instantly. Their eyes met.

This time he took her hand in his. "So what do you say, Armstrong? You want to try again?"

She glanced at their entwined fingers. She thought about all the hurt he'd caused her, then she thought about the pure hell her life had been without him. The decision proved to be no decision, after all. "We'll probably kill each other," she told him with a small smile.

"Probably," he agreed.

She sighed. "And I'm still not sure how much we have in common."

"There is that."

She grinned. "But what the hell, you only live once, right?"

In return, he squeezed her hand, then rose from the bed.

"Hey, where you going?" Cassie called after him, startled by his abrupt leave-taking.

"To pass out."

He looked as if he just might. Between his swollen eye and his slight limp from the encounter with the door, Charlie had definitely not gotten the better of this exchange.

She hid a smile. "Well, don't I at least get a kiss?"

He turned to her, eyes filled with mock terror. "No way, tiger. You've already done enough damage tonight." Hand on the doorknob, he grinned. "Don't worry, by tomorrow I'll be back to fighting form."

Laughing, she watched him leave the room.

7

EARLY the following morning, Cassie was awakened by a smart rat-a-tat-tat on her hotel door. She knew who was on the other side even before she glanced through the peephole. This time, she threw open the door, her smile welcoming and bright, suspiciously bright for a woman who'd had only a few hours of sleep. "Charlie Whitman, as I live and breath. What a surprise."

He stepped into the room and shut the door with finality before sweeping her into his arms.

Back to fighting form, as promised, Charlie Whitman was as outrageous as ever. She wouldn't have had him any other way.

"Excuse me," he said politely, "but there's something I forgot to do last night. And be warned, I plan to make up for lost time." His lips zeroed in on hers.

Her laughter died in her throat as she got a good look at his face, and instead of kissing him, she stepped back. Her hands crept to her mouth, muffling her horrified words. "Oh, my God, Charlie. Your eye."

Charlie did indeed sport a beauty of a shiner. For a guy with an eye that looked the way his did, he was surprisingly lighthearted about the whole thing. Unconcernedly, he tapped the swollen area. "What, this? I don't know, I kind of like it." Of course, he might have liked Godzilla this morning, that's how happy he was. "I think it gives me a certain raffish charm. A more mature look. You know, more Captain Hook than Peter Pan."

"Or Patches, the RCA dog."

The words slipped out before Cassie could stop them, and she was instantly contrite. "Oh, Charlie, I'm sorry. I didn't mean that. I shouldn't have said it." Especially since it was her fault.

The apology came a little too late. "Are you teasing me, Armstrong? Because you know I always get even." He advanced a threatening step.

Yes, she knew he always did. Just as she knew their relationship was back on track. She couldn't quite control the bright smile of happiness that lit her face even as she held out her empty hands. "Sorry, Charlie. No clipboard to steal this time."

"I have other ways of getting even," he told her with a grin.

She didn't retreat. "Is that right? Like what?"

He crooked an index finger. "C'mere and I'll show you."

Needing no further urging, she slipped into the circle of his arms, settling her hands behind his back, sighing when he locked his arms around her waist and drew her even closer. No retreat possible, but retreating was the farthest thing from her mind.

His hand moved from her waist to cradle the soft fall of her hair, and inexorably he brought her lips closer. "That's what I like," he breathed. "A woman who takes her punishment willingly."

"I'm the one with a great right jab, remember?" She sighed. But her tough talk proved only an illusion as his lips claimed hers.

Some things never changed. Like the teasing undercurrent that marked their relationship and the magic between them whenever they were together. There was a sense of rightness about being in each other's arms. The hotel room faded into oblivion, the Majik Toy account was forgotten, and the misery of the last few weeks was erased as they saw, felt, touched and breathed each other.

Charlie kissed her to make up for the long separation and for the hurt he'd caused and also for the blind, selfish fool that he'd been. Passion overcame logic, understanding triumphed over hurt, and the kiss they shared was all the more potent for the test they had endured.

How could he have ever let her go?

How could she have ever imagined herself indifferent to him?

What started out as a simple caress soon escalated into a heated embrace as they fed the fire that burned hotly between them even when they'd tried to deny it.

Charlie sought to make up for lost time. Cassie was still clad in her shortie nightgown, and he moved his hand from her hair to the rounded fullness of her breast, exposed to his touch by her arms tightly wound around his neck. Gently, he cupped the vulnerable flesh, realizing how long he'd wanted to do this.

Beneath the sinuous silk of her gown, her nipples grew taut at the light touch, but as a groan escaped her lips, she tried to damp the fire that was raging out of control between them. Lost to mindless pleasure, it took all her considerable willpower to stay his hand, particularly when his lips turned to nuzzle the soft skin of her neck.

Unlike the first time on that snowy winter's eve not so long ago, it was Cassie who pulled away first. "Whitman." She sighed. "We can't do this now. We have a dining room full of people waiting for us, not to mention a campaign to plan."

She was right, of course, but he couldn't seem to make himself let go of her. Couldn't seem to get enough of her. It wasn't just sex he wanted from her, he realized with a small jolt of surprise, it was also the comfort of her.

Cradling her in his arms, he rested his forehead against hers, wanting to maintain their closeness, needing the warm security of her. The need to be close was a first for Charlie Whitman. Security. Closeness. A sense of belonging. These were things he'd never found anywhere else, never found with anyone else. Certainly not within his family. He had told himself he didn't need them, didn't want them. But now he suspected he'd been too afraid to let anyone get near, too afraid they'd hurt him. The truth was, he couldn't help but be a little afraid. Old habits died hard. As always, even now, Charlie Whitman felt the need to cover himself, just in case.

"So, Armstrong," he heard himself say. "Any second thoughts about this? Speak now or forever hold your piece." He spoke lightly, but his feelings weren't light, and he was almost scared to look into her eyes, afraid of the rejection he might read there.

Those blue eyes met his steadfastly, convincing him better than words could. He read passion in her expression, yes, but also caring and kindness and a steadfastness that Charlie had always lacked in his passion-on-the-run, hurt-you-before-you-hurt-me relationships with other women.

He saw courage, too. She had the courage to try again, but also the strength to put him to the test. "I think, Charlie Whitman, I should be asking you that question. So here goes. Any second thoughts, Charlie? Speak now or forever hold your piece."

When he answered, it was with the truth. "Not a one." Suddenly his eyes danced boyishly. "Want me to prove it?" He zeroed in for another kiss, but this time Cassie sought to evade him. Laughing, she twisted away. "Not now, Charlie. Duty calls, I'm afraid."

There was still something Charlie needed to say, and wanting her to take it the right way, he chose his next words carefully. He reached out and took her hands. Seeing his serious expression, Cassie stopped laughing. What now? She held her breath.

He forced himself to look at her, took a deep breath. "Cassie, I'm not very good at this relationship business." He almost stumbled over the words, but made himself go on, knowing it was important. "And I, ah, just think we should take it slow this time."

His expression changed once again. "God, did I just say that? To a half-naked woman when we're alone in a hotel room? Oh, how the mighty have fallen. What are you doing to me, Cassie Armstrong?"

She knew exactly what she was doing, exactly what he was doing. And even as she laughed, she held out her hand. "To going slow."

Smiling, Charlie sealed the deal with a shake.

"And, since we've decided to go slow," Cassie concluded with a sigh, "maybe you'd better leave now while I get dressed. How about if I meet you in the dining room in ten minutes?"

She was right again, of course. She usually was, he was finding out. But that didn't make it any easier to leave. With one final longing look at Cassie's partially clad form, he reluctantly started toward the door. Still, he couldn't help but grumble at the threshold. "God, this maturity business is hell." She pushed him out with a small smile and locked the door.

AROUND THE breakfast table, the assembled cast focused on Charlie's black eye. All except Cassie Armstrong, of course, who studied the menu as if her life depended upon the choice between eggs or pancakes.

For the longest time no one said a word, until finally Scott, the account executive, took the plunge.

"What the hell happened to you?"

"MYOB," Joe warned, in Joe shorthand.

Scott's eyes flashed. "What are we supposed to do, sit here and pretend not to notice his shiner?"

"It's okay, Joe," Charlie soothed. "A small misunderstanding," he informed the group smoothly. Then he grinned, reaching across the table for Cassie's hand. "But worth it. Right, Armstrong?"

She beamed. "Whatever you say, Charlie."

When Cassie placed her hand in his, a collective sigh of relief went up around the table.

"Well, thank God," Scott muttered, attacking his grapefruit. "Maybe we can finally get some work done around here."

Before they'd finished their meal, they were interrupted, this time by the dining room hostess bearing a phone.

"Tom Garnett? Mr. Tom Garnett?"

The research director grabbed the phone, then blanched at the news on the other end.

"The baby," Cassie breathed. "His wife must be in labor."

She was right. "Gotta run," Tom announced, throwing down his napkin as he sprang from the table. "It's show time." His face bore the nervous excitement and fear of any first-time father.

"Don't worry about your luggage," Cassie called after him. "We'll take care of it. Just go...and good luck."

"Good luck," they all echoed, watching Tom dash from the room.

"Well, it looks like there's going to be happy endings all the way around, huh, Armstrong?" Charlie said, lounging against the counter as she paid the breakfast bill with the agency credit card.

"So it seems. Now all we have left to do is figure out a campaign for Majik Toys." No small feat at the eleventh hour.

For a woman who worried as much as Cassie normally did, she was surprisingly lighthearted. With Charlie at her side, she felt invincible, as if she could leap tall buildings in a single bound, and she suspected he felt the same. As they walked through the hotel lobby toward the conference room, their hands just seemed to join. She wasn't even sure who had initiated the contact. But the need to touch came often and frequently, and they indulged after the long weeks apart. Still, Cassie couldn't help but notice the curious looks passersby gave Charlie's eye and couldn't help but feel a little guilty about the events of last night, happy ending notwithstanding.

"I am sorry about the shiner, Charlie. I still can't believe I did that. Not that you didn't deserve it, of course. But I'm sorry. Does it hurt?"

Swinging their joined hands between them, he cast her a teasing look. "You wouldn't happen to have a bullet handy to bite on, would you? Or better yet . . ." That devilish light entered his eyes. "Kiss it and make it better. Here, I'll even make it easy for you." He stooped to her level, presenting his injured eye.

She tried to appear stern, no easy task when her heart was singing with happiness. "This is a public place, Whitman. And I'm the reserved type, remember? No public displays of affection."

Affection, Charlie thought. Another unfamiliar word to add to his growing vocabulary. This seemed to be his day for firsts. And yet, he realized that affection was exactly what he felt for her—affection intertwined with passion. It was a powerful combination.

He caught her blush, and that small involuntary response only increased the feelings he had for her. "Is that why you're glinting with rage again? Come on, Armstrong," he cajoled. "You owe it to me. I'm a soldier wounded in battle. I promise I won't even touch you."

Laughing, cheeks pink, she tried to peck him on the brow, but he abruptly changed tactics, sweeping his arms around her and lifting her clear off the floor.

"You lied, Charlie Whitman," she accused, trying to remain stern but losing the battle as laughter crept into her eyes. "Now put me down. Everybody's looking at us."

They were. Harried businesspeople, armed with briefcases, stopped to stare at the sight of a laughing woman in the arms of a man with a black eye. But they only paused for a moment before they smiled. All the world loves a lover and it was evident, even to the casual passerby, that that's what these two people were.

"And do you care?" Charlie asked.

She sighed, and her lips met his.

There was no telling where it might have gone had not Joe Mancini abruptly materialized. Wordlessly, he pulled Cassie from Charlie's arms and strong-armed them into their conference room as they shared bemused glances. "Work," he told them, accentuating his point in true Joe fashion by slamming the door.

And work they did. The hours blurred, lunch into dinner, dinner into evening and finally night. Of the four stalwart remaining souls, no one left the room the entire day as they brainstormed and argued, bringing up strategies and then rejecting them. Sometime in the wee hours of the morning, Scott and Joe begged off, claiming exhaustion. But Cassie and Charlie refused to give up. Ignoring their pounding headaches and aching limbs, they argued on.

Legs stretched out on a chair to relieve cramped muscles, Cassie sipped a cup from what had to be her third pot of coffee of the day. Even her taste buds must have retired for the night, she decided, for she barely tasted it. She watched as Charlie restlessly paced the room, up one side and down the other, like a laboratory rat caught in a maze. After so many hours, she was surprised he still had the energy.

She threw down her pen. "I don't know, Charlie," she sighed. "We've been over this and over this. There's nothing here to work with. Other than being premium-priced, there's nothing that stands out about this line of toys. There's just no unique selling proposition. I'm beginning to think we're wasting our time."

But Charlie Whitman worked with a tenacity that caught Cassie by surprise. It was no wonder he was so good at what he did; he simply chose not to lose. "Do you want to let Vince think he was right?" he demanded. "Well, do you?"

Sighing, Cassie picked up her pen again.

As tired as he was, he paced faster, running a hand distractedly through his already rumpled hair. "There's got to be something," he insisted. "I mean, why are they selling so many toys? How about a heritage strategy? Majik's been in business a long time."

"And who cares?" Cassie countered. "Kids don't give a hoot that Majik was founded in 1911, and we know the appeal has to be kid-driven. And besides—" she sighed "—we've already been over this."

He conceded the point, but stubbornly persisted. "Okay, okay. Well then, how about the premium-priced angle? You know, you deserve the best."

She shot that down, as well. "Same problem. Besides, a competitor is already using that idea, and none too successfully, I might add." She stretched wearily. "I'm sorry to be a quitter, Charlie, but face it. There's nothing to say about this line of toys."

His shoulders slumped wearily. "I guess you're—" The words of agreement died in his throat. Suddenly he stopped pacing, his eyes shooting toward hers. "Wait a minute. Wait a minute. Back up a minute. What did you just say?"

She was so tired, she could barely remember her own name, never mind a careless remark. She shrugged. "I don't know. I guess I said there's nothing to say."

Charlie stood straighter. "That's it. My God, it's so simple. It's been staring us in the face all along. Armstrong, you are brilliant. Absolutely brilliant."

"Well, of course, I am..." With his hair rumpled and his eyes blurry and red, not to mention black-and-blue, he looked suddenly like some mad scientist. For an instant, she feared Charlie Whitman had snapped under the strain. "What are you talking about?"

"Armstrong, what is the first rule of advertising?"

She stared at him uncertainly even as she dutifully replied, "If you can't beat them with your brains, then baffle them with your bull."

"True, true." Charlie grinned, energized. "Okay, then what's the second rule of advertising?"

"If you have nothing to say, then sing it." And then she stopped as it hit her, too. "Oh, my God, that's it. You're right." Catching the fever, she sat up straight in her chair. "A commercial with no words."

"Exactly." Charlie grinned. "Just a montage of the Majik Toy line. Set against a theme song like—like..." Thinking aloud, he gestured with his hands.

"'This Magic Moment,'" Cassie supplied for him after a beat.

"Right," Charlie agreed. Like all great ideas this one built slowly, piece by piece, each piece a vital part of the formula.

"And then with a tag line of..." She glanced at Charlie now.

"Share the Majik," he finished. "Superimposed on the screen in bold-face type and spelled just like the company name, to reinforce the brand image."

Across the length of the room, they stared at one another, unable to believe what they'd just done. And then in a flash, they were in one another's arms. Hugging and jumping up and down like children, they congratulated each other. "My God, we did it! We really did it!"

"It's brilliant," Cassie said. "The appeal is perfect for kids, and we can use a doughnut in the music to allow for promotions. It works for the whole product line. And it's not hard sell, so the parents can't object."

"And," Charlie concluded triumphantly, "the best part is, even Vince will understand it. No words to confuse him."

Laughing, they shared a quick kiss before Charlie broke away. "Save that thought," he told her with a reluctant grin. "What time is it?"

Cassie glanced at her watch. "Three o'clock. That gives us eight hours until presentation time. It will take us an hour to get back to the city even if we break all local speed limits."

"Time is of the essence, Armstrong, but we can do it. Let's wake up the others." But Cassie was already way ahead of him, dashing toward the door.

"Joe can get started on the storyboards," she yelled over her shoulder.

"Right," Charlie agreed, on her heels. "Scott can head down to New York and locate the tape in a twenty-four-hour music store. That's a perfect assignment for him."

Somehow, some way, they pulled it off. Joe finished the storyboards in lightning-quick speed, Charlie drove like a madman, and Cassie kept a sharp lookout for less-than-understanding police officers. The lush Westchester landscape zoomed by in a dizzying blur, which soon turned into the less-than-lush concrete pavement of the Bronx. Charlie swerved in and out of lanes, tailgating along with the best of them. Knuckles white with strain, Cassie couldn't help but ask, "Where did you learn to drive, Whitman? The Indy 500?"

"Manhattan," he told her with a grin. "Same difference." He spared her a look, smiling at her expression and the way she instinctively braked on the passenger side, as if that would do her any good. "But you know, you don't make a bad point guy yourself. If I ever turn to a life of crime, remind me to bring you along."

She blanched as he barely missed colliding with a slow-moving tractor trailer, not quite able to suppress a gasp when he squeezed into another lane. "No jokes now, Whitman," she pleaded. "Just watch the road."

"Yes, Bonnie," he replied dutifully, grinning as his attention returned to the Roman chariot race that marked the New York road system during rush hour.

It seemed the angels were smiling on them this morning, for somehow they arrived all in one piece, and just in the nick of time. Screeching into the city on two wheels, they shuddered to a halt in front of the Majik Toy building at the stroke of eleven o'clock, the witching hour. The car was still knocking with postignition and protested strain when they leaped out, conveniently ignoring the No Parking Anytime sign. They found a triumphant Scott in the lobby, waving the tape he'd found. The foursome rode up to the executive floor.

In the end, it was all worth it. Just as they'd predicted, Vince Bertolli loved the campaign, and even understood it, with no silly words to confuse him. But Vince, being Vince, seemed even more intrigued by

Charlie's black eye, or more to the point, that Cassie had given it to him.

"You got chutzpah, kid," he congratulated her, bestowing upon her his highest accolade. "The kind of broad I want on my side. You got my business for as long as you want it."

Cassie's eyes widened at the term *broad* and Charlie struggled unsuccessfully to hide a laugh as they shook hands all around.

They had saved the account, beaten back the forces of darkness. It wasn't exactly keeping the world safe for democracy, but in the advertising business that was about as good as it got. Hailed at the agency as conquering heroes, they were greeted with another piece of news. The Garnetts had an infant daughter, weighing in at eight pounds, six ounces.

It was a morning of triumph all the way around.

Finally alone in her office, Cassie and Charlie, in each other's arms, shared a kiss.

"Well, let's see, Armstrong," he said with a smile. "So far in the last few days, you've punched a man, saved an account and survived the Indy 500."

"Not to mention," Cassie added, "being called a broad, and one with chutzpah, at that." She couldn't resist teasing him. "Is that what you meant by taking it slow, Charlie Whitman? Because I'd certainly hate to see you move fast."

"Any regrets?" he had to ask.

"None," she answered promptly. And then she laughed. "But life with you is certainly not dull."

8

As MUSICIANS STROLLED and waiters hovered, Charlie clicked his champagne flute against Cassie's. "To our six-week anniversary, Armstrong. I made it."

Catching her laugh, he grinned. "Okay, it's not gold, it's not even wood, but for me, that's pretty good."

"You're doing very well, Charlie." And he was.

As April burst into May, they were spending all their time together. Though Cassie had worried about being involved with a co-worker, her relationship with Charlie outside the office had only enhanced their professional life. As for Charlie, he would have thought all this togetherness would make him feel trapped, and six months ago, even three months ago, it probably would have. But now, the more he saw of Cassie, the more he wanted to see her. Though they'd never talked about it, neither dated anyone else. Neither wanted to.

Charlie raised his glass again in salute. "To going slow."

Glass at her mouth, Cassie sipped, then paused. "Maybe we're going too slow, Charlie."

For all their closeness, for all the time they'd spent together, they still hadn't made love.

Charlie's gray eyes darkened. But he didn't say a word. Though he would have died rather than admit it, he was a little afraid. He knew Cassie well by now, knew it was not the kind of thing she took easily or lightly. And now, neither did he.

She knew him every bit as well as he knew her. Those blue eyes were very bright. "Let's go to your place tonight, Charlie."

"It's a mess," he warned.

She wasn't a woman to back down. "I won't even notice."

Need overcame caution. Tossing down several bills, he hustled her out into the night. Laughing, she tugged against his urgent grip. "We could have had dinner. I'm not in that much of a hurry."

"I am." Those gray eyes smiled at her, and even as he hailed a cab, he claimed her mouth in a kiss.

"Oh," she murmured, breath strangled in her throat. Leaning against him weakly, she swallowed hard. "I wasn't very hungry anyway."

"OH," SHE SAID AGAIN, but this time for an entirely different reason. Hovering at the threshold of Charlie's SoHo apartment, she couldn't seem to manage more as she simply stared.

Charlie Whitman had said it was a mess. Charlie Whitman was a master of understatement.

Seeing the place through her eyes, he winced. "The cleaning lady canceled out on me," he explained, grabbing a mateless sock that had somehow found its way to the foyer floor. Not knowing what else to do it with it, he stuffed it into his pants pocket. Unfortunately an errant beer can wouldn't fit as readily.

Watching him, Cassie was touched. "You know, Charlie, maybe your cleaning lady didn't cancel. Maybe she died and is buried in here somewhere."

"Are you teasing me, Armstrong? How many times do I have to tell you that I have ways of getting even?"

"Prove it."

Eyes dancing with delight, he did, then rested his chin against the softness of her hair. "Are you sure the mess doesn't bother you?"

"Well . . ." With a laugh, she looked around. Despite the chaos, she liked what she saw. The eclectic architecture of the SoHo loft, with its wide-open spaces and exposed beams, suited its owner to a tee. She liked it almost as much as she liked Charlie Whitman. Which was a lot.

Taking him by the hand, all the while smiling at him, she led him over to the sofa, laughed again when Charlie had to clear off two weeks of accumulated debris.

"My remote," he muttered. "I've been looking all over for this thing. You are a good influence, Armstrong."

"You've influenced me, too," she said.

With that bright smile in her eyes, she gently pushed him down. Charlie let himself be taken. Cassie Armstrong was a woman of many surprises. Nice surprises.

"Be gentle with me, Armstrong," he joked.

"Not a chance."

"God, I love tough women."

How much, he was only beginning to figure out, especially when her fingers strayed to the buttons of his shirt and purposefully opened them one by one. In that instant, he couldn't help but think of what a contrast she was. Vulnerable and yet powerful.

And Cassie was feeling both at the moment.

Laughter forgotten, he reached out to draw her mouth near.

Her skin tingled and warmed beneath Charlie's gentle touch. She felt relaxed and supercharged at the same time, and she sighed as his fingers gently probed her vulnerable nape, easing away tension while creating some anew. She had never been quite so aware of her body before, what could be done to it and what it could do.

As if with a mind of its own, his hand eased up the silk of her shirt to feel the warmth of her skin against his own. Hardened calluses against soft creamy flesh. A new exercise in torture and delight. He could almost feel her melting beneath his fingertips, fluid and yet resilient, too. Her muscles tightened, then relaxed under his caressing touch. His mouth sought her flesh, tasting honeysuckle enhanced by the earthy cleanliness of sweat.

When she purred in delight, his hand quested toward her breasts. Through the confines of her bra, he circled the nipple with a light touch, marveling when it sprang taut as if with a life force of its own.

Charlie was past all coherent thought when he unclasped her bra, fumbling in his growing excitement. Where he'd always possessed such expertise, he was now all thumbs. Cassie reached behind her to help him. Her breasts sprang free.

He kneaded their fullness, trying to keep it gentle, but soon losing the battle as he bent over to tease them with his tongue.

No words passed between them; they didn't need any now. Their bodies were saying everything.

Mindless with pleasure, heedless with sensation, she tugged off his shirt and tossed it carelessly on the floor, then proceeded to remove her own, sending it along with her bra to the floor. She wrapped an arm around his neck and pulled him down to rest full length against her, delighting in his weight, the way his chest hairs sensuously rubbed against her exposed breasts. In that act, she proved she was his equal, if not his master. "Better," she breathed, opening her mouth to receive his kiss.

He pulled back to stare into her eyes, and something he saw there stopped him.

With the last vestiges of sanity, he held back.

"What's the matter, Charlie?"

"I, ah..." For a man who made his living with words, why was he finding the next few so difficult?

Seeing his troubled face, Cassie guessed at the problem. "I'm not exactly a virgin, Charlie," she ventured gently.

With a ghost of a grin, he replied, "Neither am I."

"And I am using something."

"It's not that, either." He released a frustrated sigh, one she matched as she stared at him.

"You're not afraid I won't respect you in the morning, are you?"

For once he failed to see the humor in the situation. "Yes. No. Oh, hell, I don't know. I don't even know what I'm saying anymore." Why was he doing this? He had a willing woman in his arms and, heaven knew, *he* was willing, so why did he feel this need to explain himself? Why not just press on and let what happened happen? A roll of the dice. A crapshoot. The way he'd always lived his life, with no thought for the future and even less for the consequences of his actions.

The answer to this question came right on its heels — because he liked Cassie Armstrong. He liked her as a person. She wasn't just a warm body to him, or an object of desire. She was a person, one with feelings and vulnerabilities. And because he cared about her, he couldn't just let the chips fall where they may.

Struggling up on one elbow, he gently traced the line of her nose, the sweep of her cheek. The steadfastness of her gaze gave him the confidence to continue. "Armstrong," he whispered. "I'm not exactly sure where this thing between us is going, and given my track record . . . Well, it's just that I don't want to hurt you again, and I don't want to get hurt."

That's when she knew she loved him. It was funny, really. She'd been attracted to him when he played the outrageous clown. She'd missed his laughing antics when they were apart. But there was more to Charlie Whitman than that, much more. There was a whole vulnerable side he'd tried to hide from the world, but little glimpses always peeked through. Like now. And it was this vulnerable Charlie that Cassie loved. The sensitive man who lurked beneath the laughing eyes of the jester. The guy who wanted to protect her, even if it meant protecting her from him. She didn't know much about Charlie's childhood, but from the little he'd told her, she knew he'd been hurt badly. She loved him for having the strength to try again and for being a little bit scared of the magnitude of the feelings between them. She'd thought they were opposites, but in this they were the same. Charlie Whitman was not taking the growing feelings between them any more lightly than she was. Being in love was a scary thing. It meant being open and exposed.

Which was exactly the way Charlie felt right now. "Cassie, do you understand what I'm trying to say?"

"Yes." But what could she tell him? That life held no guarantees? That sometimes you just had to trust your instincts and jump right in? And how amazing it was that it was she who had to tell this man, of all people, that. Yet somehow it made sense. In all relationships, at least good ones, partners changed roles, sometimes giving, sometimes receiving, and sometimes, when one drew back, the other had to press forward. Which was exactly what Cassie was doing now.

"And?"

She met his eye and answered the only way she could. "Charlie Whitman, has anyone ever told you that you worry too much?"

Whatever he expected her to say, that wasn't it. When he started to grin, she grinned right back. "Are you teasing me again, Armstrong?"

"Not at all, Charlie Whitman. In fact, I am trying to seduce you. And, I might add, you are not being very helpful."

"I think I can remedy that." Not teasing, he lowered his lips to hers.

And remedy it he did.

When she'd imagined her first romantic interlude with Charlie—and she realized now just how often she'd imagined it—she'd pictured soft lights and satin sheets, Charlie being the proficient lover she'd always imagined him to be.

But in life, things rarely worked out the way you'd imagined. And since nothing in Charlie and Cassie's whirlwind courtship had gone according to strictly held convention, neither did their first joining. It happened then and there in Charlie's less-than-immaculate living room, on his less-than-immaculate sofa.

It wasn't the way Charlie had imagined it, either. He'd wanted the first time to be gentle and romantic, a slow-building seduction of the senses. Instead it was a hot molten ride into the beyond and back.

He wanted to be gentle, he wanted to savor each and every caress, but he couldn't seem to control this any more than he could control his feelings.

His mouth moved from her lips to her breasts. He nuzzled the hollow between them, her skin salty and slick to the touch. *Slow down,* his mind commanded. But Cassie's fingers dug into his shoulders, almost gouging him in her passion, and instead of slowing down, his mouth feasted.

Zippers rasped in the quiet of the room as they struggled against clothes, desperate now to touch, to taste and to possess.

An iota of sanity returned. "Cassie, wait a minute. Let me . . ."

But he never finished the thought.

When Cassie Armstrong committed to something, she committed all the way. She might be slow to make up her mind, but when she did, she did nothing by half measure, this included.

She was hot and slick and ready, and at the mere touch of him, she jolted into orgasm, her first but by no means her last, for as he reached the same pinnacle, in that same place of mindless being, where nothing else seemed to matter, she cried out again. "Charlie!" Just that one word said it all.

They drifted back to reality by inches. Even as dusk stole through the apartment, bathing them in a rosy light, even as the room grew cooler and the hard floor grew harder, Cassie didn't notice. Her head nestled on Charlie's shoulder, she lay half-prone against him while he toyed lazily with her hair. She could almost feel him smile through the darkness, that's how attuned they were to each other.

"How do you feel, Armstrong?" he asked.

"Pretty good," she managed, surprised she was capable of speech at all, even more surprised that she was not embarrassed in the least after having attacked him the way she did. "How 'bout you?"

"Cheap, sweaty and used." She felt rather than saw the rumble of laughter from his chest, sighed lazily when he rolled over her to kiss her again. "Thank you."

He stared down into those blue eyes. "Was it...?" He paused. He was not really going to go for the oldest cliché in the world, was he? He was not actually going to ask her if it was good for her?

Even without the words, she seemed to know what he was asking. She debated saying it, wondering if it would go right to his head and doubting that Charlie Whitman needed any reassurance in this department. Then again, if she wanted him to open up and be vulnerable, she had to do the same. "My first," she told him, though shyly now.

But Charlie seemed more pleased than smug. "Really?"

"Really."

Those gray eyes danced, not with mischief but with myriad emotions too complicated to put into words. "You know," he told her, "I think I can do even better."

And amazingly enough, he did.

Hunger of a different sort finally drove them from their cozy nest on the floor.

Leaning over to kiss her brow, he murmured against her lips, "The least I can do is feed you, after I've ravished you twice."

She looped her arms around his neck, too lazy to move, too replete with happiness to want to move ever again. She wanted this moment to go on and on. "Is that what you did? Ravish me? Seems to me I helped."

It seemed so to him, too. Another surprise from Ms. Cassie Armstrong. She might not be all that experienced, but what she lacked in expertise she made up for with enthusiasm. And the more she gave, the more he wanted to give back. Giving instead of taking—another first, and a little scary for a man thirty-six years old who thought he knew all there was to know about pleasures of the flesh.

Her hand moved to play with a curly hair on his chest, and he caught her fingers. "Armstrong," he warned with grin, "if we don't get up now, we probably never will."

She conceded that point with a grin, groaning when he got to his feet. As he started toward the kitchen, she lingered long enough to slip on her silk shirt. Ridiculous, she thought, after what they'd shared, but just for good measure she grabbed his pants, too, which he seemed to have conveniently forgotten.

As she wandered into the kitchen and he caught sight of the T-shirt and his pants in her hand, he had to laugh. Several clichés sprang to mind, one of which had to do with locking barn doors, but he never uttered a one.

Intercepting his look, she stared him down. "Don't you tease me, Charlie Whitman. I know it's silly but..." She threw his pants at him. "Humor me. Put them on."

He did, all the while grinning at her chagrined expression and the way she refused to look any lower than his eyes.

The slight blush on her face had him crossing the room toward her, and the exciting dichotomy of enthusiastic lover and shy ingenue had him cupping her chin in his hand and asking the next question. "Are you going to stay over tonight?"

The question caught them equally by surprise.

He had never asked a woman to stay the night at his apartment before, had never wanted one to. He preferred to control the situation, orchestrating his own leave-taking. As Fran had once accused him, he was always the life of the party, but rarely very good at the morning after.

Cassie was uncertain. "Do you want me to?"

He hesitated at this critical juncture, not wanting to be vulnerable and yet remembering all she'd put on the line, and the cagey response, 'Well, do you want to?' went unsaid. "Yeah," he muttered, "I do."

It wasn't exactly an impassioned declaration, it certainly wasn't "I love you," but the huskily muttered words touched Cassie all the more because she understood their cost and their cause. Calmly, she met his eyes. "Good, then I'll stay."

He remembered to breathe then, wondering how she could smile at him so calmly when his heart raced as if he'd just run the Boston Marathon. "Well, then, great. I guess that's settled." He looked around the kitchen as if somewhat surprised to find himself there. "So what would you like to eat? I have some eggs, I think. Or there's . . ."

She saw his confusion. She held his eye. "I'm not really very hungry."

"Funny," he said, grinning, suddenly more sure of himself. "Neither am I. You know, you haven't even seen the bedroom yet. I do have one, you know, although you probably don't believe me. And it's even got a bed. Even us bohemians in SoHo go for the amenities sometimes."

"You're right," Cassie teased. "I don't believe you. Prove it."

Lifting her in his arms, he carried her up the spiral staircase to the loft. He whispered, "I told you these clothes were a waste of time, Armstrong."

MORNING, Charlie thought, as the first pale pink rays of the sun peeked through the skylight. He had made it to morning. And how did he feel on this momentous occasion. Trapped? Claustrophobic?

No, he thought with a grin. A little achy, maybe, from all the strenuous activities of the night before. Very tired, which was hardly news since they'd barely closed their eyes. But definitely not trapped, certainly not claustrophobic.

He glanced at the woman slumbering peacefully next to him in the brass bed, smiling at the glow in her cheeks, the tumble of caramel-colored hair spread out like a cloud against the pillow. Almost absently, he toyed with a lock.

Is this love? he wondered. *Is that what this strange feeling is?* Having never felt it before, he couldn't be quite sure, and yet he thought it just might be. He wasn't afraid. Tentative, maybe, hopeful, definitely. But not afraid.

It was almost as if she'd sensed the intensity of his thoughts, for her eyes drifted open, full of wonder and sleepy contentment. At his thoughtful expression, those eyes widened and she asked, "What's the matter?"

"Nothing," he answered. "Absolutely nothing." And for the space of that moment it was true.

He almost told her then, almost confessed his growing feelings aloud, but something held him back. Maybe the fact that everyone always said it in bed. Or maybe because he wasn't really sure what he was feeling, or maybe because he was still a little afraid.

Reading his expression, she told herself she didn't need the words. They would come.

ON MONDAY MORNING, Cassie floated into the agency on a cloud of happiness.

"I had a wonderful weekend," she informed Fran.

Above her conference report, Fran's eyes narrowed. "So I see."

"What's wrong? Did you and Joe have a fight or something?"

"No. No. In fact, everything's fine. Wonderful, actually." As if in spite of herself, a softer expression crept into Fran's eyes and then she pushed herself back from the desk. "If you'll excuse me, I have to go see a man about something."

Fran marched into Charlie's office without knocking, and he took one look at the thunderous expression on her face and immediately started defending himself. "I handed in the assignment. I swear. It wasn't even late."

Fran stared him down. "Hurt her and I'll kill you."

There was no doubt about the who in question here, nor about Fran's motives. Cassie Armstrong aroused protective instincts in everyone she met, Charlie included.

Being a woman who always liked to have the last word and one who knew how make an exit, Fran marched herself out just as abruptly as she'd come, but the warning lingered.

That night, alone in his apartment, Charlie pulled out his manuscript. With a thoughtful sigh, he started to type again.

9

LOVING CHARLIE WHITMAN was a little like walking a tightrope. When you were on top, you were on top of the world, but you always knew it was a long way down. Cassie was happy, happier than she'd ever been in her life, and she knew Charlie was happy, as well. More and more, they were becoming a couple. Her things found their way into his apartment and his into hers, their two lives comingling. Charlie was unlike any man she'd ever met, more complex than any man she'd ever met. The more she knew him, the more she found to know about him. Like peeling an onion, each uncovered layer revealed another layer. He could be the laughing life of the party, the tender lover and even the man of mystery. For all that, Cassie was conscious that Charlie held a part of himself back. Not only because he wouldn't put his feelings into words, but in other ways, as well. Finding his manuscript confirmed it.

She'd been looking for a pen, which in Charlie's apartment was akin to the quest for the Holy Grail. Rummaging in his desk drawers, she'd unearthed a sheaf of typed pages. Without meaning to pry, she read the title page, her eyes widening at the author's name and then even further at the unlikely subject. *Commitments, by Charlie Whitman.*

The urge to read the pages was strong, but sneaking was not Cassie's style. She went looking for Charlie, who was fixing a late-night snack. "I didn't know you were writing a novel!"

"I'm not." Cutlery clattered as he raced for the living room and reached for the pages. "It's just some scribbling."

Not entirely sure whether to be hurt or delighted at this new aspect of Charlie's character, she hung on. "It doesn't look like scribbling, it looks like a manuscript. Why didn't you tell me you were writing?"

"Because I'm not. Now gimme."

"Can I read it?"

"No!"

At his vehement tone her eyes widened, and suddenly she wanted nothing more in this world than to read the hundred-odd pages she clutched in her hot little hands. "Please."

He was already pulling them from her grip. "I mean, it's not very good and it's not done." He couldn't seem to write the ending, but then that was always Charlie's problem with commitments. He forced himself to smile naturally. "Now give it back, Armstrong, before I'm forced to get physical."

Much as she wanted to press the issue, she knew that Charlie Whitman could not be rushed. A teasing glint in her eye, she said, "You want it, Whitman, then come and get it."

The teasing ended up pretty much as they'd both expected. Later, lying next to him in bed, she studied his sleeping face. She thought about those unread pages and all they signified, and she wondered if Charlie Whitman would ever trust her enough to let her all the way in.

THE TELEPHONE CALL from Charlie's mother only served to illustrate how tall were Charlie's walls of defense and the reasons for them.

As New York blazed into one of the hottest summers in history, Charlie and Cassie returned to his apartment after a day at the beach. Feeling languorous and lazy from the combined effects of the summer sun and Charlie's company, she flopped down on his sofa, sighing her contentment and closing her eyes.

Charlie switched on the air conditioner, then joined her there, settling next to her and lazily cupping her face in one hand as a prelude to a kiss. Lips mere inches from hers, he paused to inquire with a grin, "Is that a blush, Armstrong, a glint of rage or a sunburn?"

The fact that Cassie's fair skin stubbornly refused to tan was a source of endless teasing for him, consternation for her and a contest between the two of them since early July when Charlie had turned a deep, dark bronze while Cassie continued to grow pinker and pinker.

One blue eye opened. "Watch it, pal. Any day now, I'm going to catch up."

Right, Charlie thought with a smile. Playing with a strap of her bathing suit, he eased it aside, pretending to admire the contrast. "You're right. It's a deep, dark Hawaiian tan. It only glows pink."

She debated mounting a defense, then abandoned the effort. "No teasing today, Charlie. It's too hot."

"Funny," he murmured. "I'm feeling kind of hot myself."

The loving between them these days was comfortable yet exhilarating. He knew her body better than she did. She loved giving herself over to pure mindless

sensation as much as she loved the teasing foreplay between them. She drew back to stare into those gray
eyes. "Just what do you have in mind, Whitman?"

"I never divulge my sneak attacks, Armstrong. You
should know that by now." But his voice had grown
husky. Moving with infinite care, he peeled down the
other strap, taking the time to kiss the flesh he'd bared,
loving it when those blue eyes darkened, when she
sighed deep in her throat.

He'd tumbled her to the couch when the phone rang.
Occupied with other more pressing matters, he could
have let it ring on into eternity, but Cassie was as conscientious as ever.

Sighing, she stayed his hand. "Shouldn't you get
that?"

"No." He punctuated the word with kisses. "I'm a
little busy right now."

He certainly was. She gasped as his lips sought her
breast. Whoever was on the other end, though, was not
giving up, either. She managed to clear her head, no
easy task when the man she loved was doing the things
she loved.

"Charlie, I gave the agency your number, and you
turned off the answering machine." She chewed her
lower lip. "Sorry, but I am expecting those mechani-
cals."

"Talk about coitus interruptus." He groaned even as
he groped for the receiver.

The instant he heard the voice on the other end, he
knew he should have trusted his instincts and let it ring.

His muscles grew rigid, and as she watched, his face
hardened. His tone grew clipped. Cassie had seen

Charlie Whitman angry, she had seen him upset, but she had never seen him like this.

He straightened on the sofa, moving away from her. Though she didn't know it at the time, it was Charlie's classic fight-or-flight response to the person on the other end. She sat up when he did, pulling up the straps of her suit.

Though Cassie had no intention of eavesdropping, before she could leave the room, before she could even get up from the sofa, she overheard Charlie's terse portion of the conversation.

"Fine. Yeah, well I've been busy. Just busy, that's all. And since when do you care what I do? When? I'm not sure if I can make it. Hey, I said I'm not sure. I'll have to get back to you. I said, I have to get back to you. Yeah, bye." And he slammed down the phone.

Though the conversation had been short to the point of rudeness, its aftermath lingered.

Wide-eyed, Cassie stared at him, dying to know who had been on the receiving end of that call, but she waited for Charlie to bring it up himself. Which he didn't do for the longest time. He stared off into space as if he'd totally forgotten her presence. And just as she was debating whether to leave, he spoke. Just one word.

"Sylvia," he said.

The name rang no bells, at least not at first. And then it hit her. "You mean your mother?"

"So my birth certificate claims," Charlie retorted. "But I'm still holding out for more proof."

Cassie tried to keep the shock from her voice, from her expression. She knew Charlie's relationship with his parents was not good—nonexistent in fact. In all the months she'd known him, he had rarely mentioned them and usually only if pressed, and then very flippantly. And for all the time she'd spent in his apartment, she had never known them to call. Clearly, though, these people were very real, and even more clearly Charlie did not feel flippant about them. Still, she had never heard anyone speak to his or her parents the way Charlie just had. She had to admit it, that came as a shock.

She thought, having talked to Fran about the subject, that she understood what it was like to grow up in a less-than-ideal family. But Fran's parents' feuds were confined between the two of them, and Fran managed to maintain a relationship with both parents, even though she couldn't respect what they did to each other. Cassie suspected that in Charlie's case the hurts went much deeper. She wasn't entirely sure how to handle this, but her heart went out to him, even as she groped for the right words.

Reading her troubled expression, he manufactured a smile. Trying to keep it light, he said, "So, where were we before we were so rudely interrupted?"

The attempt at frivolity fell as flat as his tone. The mood had been broken, a lovely day ruined. He wasn't really surprised; his parents had ruined everything in his life. Or at least they had given it the old college try.

"Charlie..." She sighed, not wanting to push, but sensing his pain. "If you ever want to talk..."

"Thanks, but there's nothing to talk about. They shouldn't have had children. Some people shouldn't. I got in their way, that's all. Period. The end. And don't look so sad, Armstrong. It happens all the time."

She supposed it did. Life was not "Leave It to Beaver" reruns, after all, not for the man she loved. Nevertheless, there was a part of her that always wanted to make things better, that believed in happily ever after.

"They invited me over for Labor Day," he said suddenly. His short laugh was a less-than-pleasant sound. "Labor Day. Fitting, huh? She claims my father's ill. Of course, living with her could account for that." He shook his head and glanced at her. "They don't know about you. Nothing personal. They wouldn't even know my telephone number if it wasn't for Information."

Feeling as if she was walking on eggs, she ventured, "Maybe you should go."

"Why? We'd only end up fighting. There'd be a nasty scene and then I'd end up walking out."

"But if your father's ill ... I don't know, Charlie. Maybe it would be different this time."

"Yeah, maybe we'll finally end up killing one another." Still, there was a part of him that hoped for better, too. The same part of him that allowed Cassie to get closer and closer. The same part of him that had tried so hard as a child. His eyes met hers. "Would you come with me?"

Now she was the one to hesitate. "I, ah, don't think I was invited."

"Please."

When he asked that way, she could refuse him nothing. In response, she slid her hand into his and squeezed. "Of course, I'll come. I mean, how bad can it be? After all, they are your parents."

10

As THE CONCRETE canyons of Manhattan gave way to the mansions and estates of Connecticut, Charlie grew tense and edgy. By the time they turned off a winding coastal road and drove through black wrought-iron gates, he was gripping the wheel with white knuckles.

Across a vast expanse of lawn, Cassie caught her first glimpse of the Whitman house. She gasped. Set against the panoramic backdrop of Long Island Sound, the Georgian manor looked like something out of *The Great Gatsby* or a movie set. When Charlie had told her his family was rich, for once he hadn't been kidding. Then again, Charlie had that break-all-the-rules, rich-kid's kind of self-confidence, the type only the truly wealthy seemed to possess. She supposed most other people were too busy trying to fit in to drop out.

Even before she met the owners, Cassie knew she was out of her element. She thought of her parents' pleasant, neat-as-a-pin Colonial saltbox with its listing front porch and the bower of roses her mother carefully and loving cultivated each year. The Whitmans could have purchased her family's home with spare change.

"Simple, yes," Cassie breathed, staring at the house as Charlie screeched to a halt on the graveled drive, "but we call it home."

Seated beside her in the rented car, he observed her awestruck expression, much like the one on his school chums' faces on the rare occasions when he'd brought them home. "Yeah, well, don't be too impressed. The Whitmans may have come over on the *Mayflower*, but they managed to lose every penny of the family fortune over the past two-hundred-odd years, thanks to bad investments and even worse genes. The money comes from old Sylvia's side of the family, and I can assure you Sylvia Judith Rothmann's clan did not ever set foot anywhere near Plymouth Rock, despite all her pretensions.

"My parents met in medical school, where they both specialized in psychiatry. One can only imagine what cruel God joined the passive and less-than-brilliant Charles Bennington Whitman III with the brilliant, social climbing and more-than-slightly eccentric Sylvia Rothmann, only child and sole inheritor of Rothmann German banking fame. Not exactly a match made in heaven, unless somebody has a fairly warped idea of the way they want to spend eternity."

And particularly not for their only child, Cassie thought. She watched Charlie open his car door, suddenly losing much of her nerve.

"Not nervous, are you?" he asked, coming around to her side of the car.

She managed a shaky laugh. "Oh, no. Of course not. Why would I be? I just wish they knew I was coming."

He cast her an enigmatic smile. "With old Sylvia, surprise tactics are usually the best. Forewarned is forearmed, as they say."

"Charlie, this isn't exactly a war."

He arched a brow. "Wanna bet?"

None of which helped Cassie's self-confidence a bit. With his hand on her arm, he escorted her to the massive front door. The door chime was answered on the first ring, dispelling the myth forever that it was difficult to get good help these days.

An elderly black woman with kind, soulful eyes and dressed in full maid's regalia directed them toward the morning room. "Thanks," Charlie replied, "but I already know the way. I'm the son."

A look of silent sympathy passed through those kind eyes before she dropped back into perfect servant mien and discreetly left them.

"No faithful family retainers around this place," Charlie whispered. "The help usually disappears at the first sight of one of my mother's infamous temper tantrums."

Temper tantrums? Cassie glanced nervously at him, but it was too late. They entered the morning room and were face-to-face with the long-awaited Whitmans.

Cassie's impression of the couple came in a confused jangle of thoughts and ideas. Of Charlie's father—older than she'd imagined and almost enfeebled despite the natty golf togs he sported. In his aquiline nose and thinning sandy hair, she could see vestiges of what an attractive man he'd undoubtedly once been. She could also see that the ravages of time, or maybe just life, had taken their toll. He must have once been a tall man, but he now had the stoop-shouldered slouch of the old, and though Charlie had inherited his father's gray eyes, what was a lively twinkle in the son's was crochety discontent in the father's.

Charlie's mother was more difficult to read. *Formidable* was the first adjective that popped to mind. A woman of indeterminate age, she was handsome rather than pretty. Her lips were too thin and her brow line too thick for her to be classified as truly beautiful. Still, there was something almost regal in her bearing—she was like a queen greeting her subjects, which seemed odd for a woman meeting her only son. In Sylvia Whitman's eyes, Cassie read keen intelligence, perhaps even cunning, together with disapproval. Sylvia's gaze flicked over the T-shirt and jeans Charlie wore defiantly, and her sniff of disdain was almost audible.

In Cassie's naïveté, and despite what Charlie had told her, she'd imagined the two psychiatrists as learned and intellectual people, maybe a little aloof, perhaps a little cool, but not cold, certainly never cruel. But there was little warmth and even less empathy in the way they welcomed their only child.

It was Charlie who stepped forward to shake his father's hand, if shake could describe the elder man's ineffectual grip. Charlie eyed his mother coolly. He didn't kiss her, didn't even address her, not that Sylvia had broken into a rendition of "Sonny Boy." As mother and son exchanged long glances, some unspoken message passed between them. They were two people who'd long ago taken each other's measure, and as the complicated, nonverbal exchange continued, Cassie's sweaty palms grew clammier.

It was Sylvia who finally broke the silence. "Well, well, so the prodigal returns." Her delivery was devoid of all warmth and all caring. Her thin lips pursed as her gaze swung to Cassie. "And who might this be?"

Charlie gritted his teeth at her condescending lady-of-the-manor tone and the way she eyed Cassie's simple summer dress, dismissing it in a glance. This visit was a mistake. "This might be Cassie," he mocked, with no further clarification. Anything he said could and would be used against him.

"What?" Charlie's father broke in. "What did you say?"

Drawing in a deep breath, Cassie stepped forward, extending her hand. "It's Cassie. Cassie Armstrong. I'm sorry to barge in on you like this. I hope you don't mind...."

Both parents ignored her outstretched hand, engaged in a private tableau of their own.

"What?" Charlie's father demanded querulously. "Who is she? What did she say? Speak up."

"Senility," Sylvia announced, contemptuously and none too quietly.

Cassie dropped her hand to her side, sparing a glance at the elder man. If he'd heard his wife, he was accustomed to comments like that, for the rheumy blue eyes showed no change in expression.

Sylvia turned her attention to Cassie. "All the Whitman men are prone to it."

Before Cassie could react, Charlie shot back, "Coming from you, Mommy dearest, I take that as a compliment."

The atmosphere in the room heated up a notch and there was no telling what might have happened next had not the maid appeared and inquired about drinks. A double, Cassie thought, a double anything. Sensing, however, that she'd need her wits about her, she settled for an iced tea. Charlie, who had no such compunctions, requested a neat whiskey, an order that evoked another raised brow from his mother.

"Thank you, Stella," Sylvia addressed the maid in her imperious tone. "But we'll eat now. Set another place and bring the drinks into the dining room."

The atmosphere did not lighten over lunch, nor did Sylvia's mood. She criticized the delicious Dover sole, she lambasted the cook for making the vinaigrette too watery and she found fault with the soundless Stella's serving style, claiming she was far too intrusive. And the most amazing thing, at least to Cassie, was that nobody seemed to find Sylvia's behavior unusual. The servants apologized and the elder Mr. Whitman ate stolidly on. Whether he truly could not hear his wife or chose to ignore her, Cassie was not sure.

By the end of the first course, Cassie's stomach was clenched, and she jumped every time Sylvia barked out an order. Down the length of the massive Jacobean rectory table, Charlie caught her eye. He raised his glass in a mocking toast, a gesture his mother intercepted.

"Well, Charlie, I see your table manners haven't improved any."

"Nor yours," he tossed back.

She pursed her lips into a tight angry line. "Don't you mock me, young man. May I remind you, I am still your mother and I gave up the best years of my life for you."

"When? What did you give up? When did you even acknowledge that I was alive?"

"You know, Charlie, I invited you here today because I'd hoped you'd grown up at last, matured, but I can see you're still the ungrateful, spoiled little brat you always were."

He set down his glass with a bang. "That's a little like the pot calling the kettle black, isn't it, Sylvia? Because you haven't changed any, either. You're still the same self-involved, controlling—"

"Delicious luncheon, Mrs. Whitman," Cassie interrupted, placing her napkin on the table. "But I'm afraid we have to go now. Right, Charlie?"

"What?" the old man complained querulously. "Blast it. What are you all yammering about? Speak up."

"Shut up, you old fool," Sylvia snapped, "before I have you committed."

Charlie shot up from his chair. "As usual, Sylvia, you've gone too far."

"Well, it's been delightful," Cassie said. "Let's all get together again soon."

Sylvia stood, as well. It was as if she was trying to prove that what Charlie had said was true, as if she couldn't bear any situation she couldn't control, any person she couldn't manipulate. She always had to have the last word, no matter the cost or the pain. She looked her son straight in the eye, her posture ramrod stiff. "I wish you'd never been born."

His mouth worked, but he held his ground. "You know something, Sylvia, for once I agree with you. I wish I'd never been born to you, either."

It was Cassie, not Charlie, who broke down. "How dare you," she choked. "How dare you say such a thing to him? How dare you even think it?"

And then Charlie was at her side, his arm on hers. "Forget it, Armstrong, you're wasting your breath. Your right hook would be more effective, except they'd press charges. Let's go."

Outside the house, Cassie hesitated by the passenger door. "Do you want me to drive?"

"No. I'm fine. I'm used to it." But he didn't look fine, and how could anyone ever get used to that? The gravel spurted beneath the tires as he peeled out of the driveway in his haste to put distance between himself and those people who called themselves his parents.

"Charlie, I'm sorry."

He laughed tonelessly. "You're sorry? For what? They're my relatives. I'm the one who should be apologizing to you."

They drove in silence after that. Cassie's heart ached for him, but she wasn't sure what to say, as if anything she could say would make it better.

Charlie didn't want to talk. He didn't want to think. He just wanted to escape, but that was his classic pattern, wasn't it? Run away. Disappear. Live to joke another day.

Suddenly, he pulled over to the side of the highway. "God," he said, choking. "If only she was an alcoholic or something. Then I could say, poor Mother, it really isn't her talking, it's the pills or the alcohol. But that's just her. You know," he confessed, "when I was a kid I used to think if I could just be good enough, smart enough, then they would love me. And then, one day when I was eight, I knew nothing I did would ever make any difference."

He still remembered that day as if it was yesterday. He could still see himself, the young Charlie Whitman, in first form at prep school, his new baseball uniform spanking clean, his cleats polished. It was his parents' first visit to the school, and he'd wanted so much to impress them. He was the star player on the team. "I had to beg them to come visit me," he remembered aloud. "They'd been fighting all morning, already locked in a cycle of fights and separations and reconciliations, as if they couldn't stand to be together but couldn't stand to be apart, either. Still, I made them come to my game. At the time I thought that home runs could fix things, make them love each other, love me. And then it was my turn at bat. . . ."

Charlie Whitman had been a good kid, the kind of kid any parent would have killed to have. Even in prep school, he'd stood heads above the crowd. Smart, athletic, handsome and eager to please, he was the best-liked boy at the whole school. Even as a youngster he'd been funny, able to make the other boys laugh.

Charlie Whitman could have been a great man, the kind of man who'd be president one day. All the elements were there. But nothing was ever good enough for Sylvia Judith Rothmann Whitman III. Certainly not her only child. She proved that once and for all on that spring afternoon in Connecticut on a baseball field.

Standing at the plate, his mouth like sawdust in his anticipation and his fear, Charlie waited for the first pitch. When it came, he swung with all his might, all his heart . . . and missed.

A gasp went up from the crowd. This was completely unexpected; Charlie was their star hitter.

Down on the field, Charlie heard only one voice, only one word: "Pathetic." He didn't hear the urgings of the others, only that single word. Without looking, without turning around, he recognized that mocking voice as his mother's.

But Charlie didn't give up. Instead he dug in deeper, tried even harder. On the second pitch, his bat met the ball with a mighty crack. As if propelled by wings, the ball sailed up into the air, wafting high and strong through that clear spring sky. The crowd went wild as he circled the bases. First, then second, then on to third. Everyone loved him and he loved himself. *There*, he thought as he started for home. He'd done it. Now they would finally love him.

Before sliding home, he paused, wanting to savor his victory. He scanned the crowd, searching for the love and approval he knew he'd find in his parents' eyes, but they were gone.

He saw them then, off in the distance, by the far side of the field. Even without hearing their words, he knew they were fighting again. He saw his father grab his mother's arm, saw her jerk away.

Everyone else at the ballpark saw it, too. The game suspended, all eyes turned to Charlie's parents, and in the silence that fell, Sylvia's words carried strongly and surely.

"And what about my career?" she shrieked. "What am I supposed to do with the little bastard? You think I want him? You keep him. He's yours."

That day he stopped trying. On that day, in that moment, something in Charlie died. He didn't cry, not then, not later. He never finished the game, just walked off the field, his head held high, and hid himself away in his room, telling himself it didn't matter. He told his coach the same same thing when he quit the team, and the headmaster when he flunked out of school. And then the next school, and the next. It didn't matter, because he didn't care. Nobody was going to hurt him again because nobody would ever get close enough again. And nobody had. Until now.

HE HAD NEVER told that story to anyone. When he looked up, Cassie's face was streaked with tears. "Oh, God, Charlie," she choked out.

He tried to make a joke of it. "Hey, forget it, Armstrong," he told her lightly. "Nobody died."

But in a sense somebody had, and Charlie did something then that he had never done in front of anyone else, would never have dreamt of doing in front of any other woman, something he had not allowed himself to do when he was eight years old. Charlie Whitman cried. He cried for the part of himself he'd lost that day, the part that was open and loving and kind. The part of him that could be vulnerable, that could trust, that could love.

With the tears came a healing.

"I love you," he cried, the words torn out of him. Even as he said them he knew they were true, knew they had been true for a long, long time. He drew in a deep breath, summoning the courage to look into her eyes. "I haven't said that to anyone since I was eight years old. Do you believe me?"

She steadfastly met his eyes. "Yes. Because I love you, too."

He smiled, wiping at his face, almost shy. "Really?"

Even through her tears, she had to smile. "Yes, really."

His response was instantaneous and sure. "Then live with me."

Now it was Cassie's turn to hesitate. She loved this man with all her heart. She knew what it had cost him to say those words. But it was not exactly the proposal she'd been hoping for, not exactly the kind of commitment she felt ready to make.

"Let me think about it," was all she could say.

11

SEVERAL AFTERNOONS LATER, Fran burst into Cassie's office. Wearing a trendy lime green pantsuit and an even louder smile, she announced dramatically, "Guess what?"

Bright happiness had transformed her friend's once cynical expression, and Cassie guessed the news even before Fran told her. Still, she played along, allowing Fran her moment.

"Well, let's see," she ventured. "You won the lottery?"

Fran's smile broadened. "Better."

"Better than winning the lottery?" Cassie snapped her fingers. "I know. I've got it. You've decided to give up advertising and do something meaningful with your life."

"Not exactly. But close. Especially the meaningful part." And then, unable to contain herself any longer, she burst out, "Joe and I are getting married! Do you believe it? Me? But look, I've got proof." From her third finger a diamond sparkled, but its luster could in no way match Fran's bedazzled smile. In that instant, she looked so much like an excited five-year-old that Cassie skirted her desk to hug her.

"Oh, Fran. That's wonderful. I know you and Joe are going to be so happy together."

Fran didn't look like a woman who needed to hear those words. "We want a big wedding," she told her friend. "With all the frills. Can you imagine me wanting all the conventional trappings? But then you only get married once, right? At least, I hope." When Cassie laughed, Fran burbled on. "Here's the rub. We only have two months to plan it. Joe doesn't want to wait, and neither do I, so I'm going to need your help. There's caterers to worry about and flowers. Not to mention photographers, and halls and . . ."

Cassie might have pointed out that for two women who routinely managed millions of dollars in advertising budgets, a wedding would be a piece of cake. But she didn't, letting Fran have her day.

As Fran went on about wedding rings and the pros and cons of long dresses versus cocktail-length styles, something closely akin to envy sliced through Cassie's heart. Not a jealous person by nature, she squashed it down. She didn't begrudge Fran her happiness. Fran, of all people, deserved this. Yet Cassie had to be truthful with herself. The romantic part of her, the part that had played wedding ever since she was a child, wished that she was in Fran's place. That it was her own wedding she was planning. The irony of the situation struck her—here the friend who'd thought she'd never find the right person was getting married, while the one who always thought she would was contemplating a far different union.

Cassie pushed the green monster of envy to the back of her mind.

"And of course," Fran continued happily, "it goes without saying that I want you for my maid of honor and Charlie for the best man. After all, we have you two to thank for all this."

Fran paused then, a question mark in her eyes. Cassie knew what her friend was asking without the words. "I've decided to live with Charlie," she said quietly.

"I see. Well, I'm happy for you, honey. You know that. And I'm sure you and Charlie will be very happy together."

Fran's expression had changed subtly and her voice lacked conviction. Cassie knew her friend was not saying what she really meant.

"But you don't approve, do you?"

"I didn't say that, Cassie."

"You didn't have to. Come on, Fran, you've always been straight with me. That's the best thing about you. So say what's on your mind. You think I'm making a mistake, don't you?"

Fran bit her lip, started to talk and then stopped. "Look, Cassie, this is none of my business."

"Fran . . ."

"Okay, just don't be mad at me, all right? Because I'm not saying any of this to hurt your feelings."

"Agreed. I promise. I won't be hurt and I won't be angry." She didn't realize how hard that promise would be to keep.

"All right. People don't change, Cassie," Fran said in a rush, before she lost her courage. "You know who told me that?"

Cassie was afraid she did. "Your mother?"

"Yeah, my mother."

"But he loves me, Fran." The words burst out before she could stop them. She realized how defensive she sounded, but she couldn't seem to stop that, either. "I know he does."

"I know he does, too, honey," Fran continued, ruthless in her good intentions. "He loves you as much as he can, he loves you as much as he's able, but with Charlie Whitman—" She shook her head "—that's all there is. Just don't expect too much of him, okay, Cassie?"

At the hurt expression that crossed Cassie's face, Fran immediately backed down. "Cassie, look, I'm sorry. I shouldn't have said anything. I'm probably wrong. You know Charlie better than anyone. And you know me, I'm a born cynic. I always think everybody's got something up their sleeve besides their arm. And as for my mother, I mean, what the hell does she know? I haven't listened to a word she's said since I was five years old, so why should you?"

Around the agency phones rang, someone shouted from the hall. Both woman ignored the chaos.

When Cassie answered, her voice was quiet. "What am I supposed to do, Fran?" she asked. "I love him and I want to be with him."

It was as simple and as complicated as that. And not even the sage, worldly Fran had any advice to offer in the face of the truth.

It was Cassie who finally broke the silence that had grown between them. "Does Charlie know? About you and Joe, that is?"

"No. We're kind of afraid to tell him, to tell you the truth. I'm not sure how Charlie is going to take the news."

Neither was Cassie. "Let me do it," she said with a sigh.

"My pleasure," Fran agreed.

After she'd left, Cassie wondered how to tell the man she loved that marriage didn't have to be a trap.

THAT NIGHT, as Cassie and Charlie walked to his apartment after work, she brought the subject up. Fall was upon them, and the air was crisp and clear, brimming with new beginnings and fresh hope. The sidewalks were once again crowded as people returned to the city from summer homes and vacation spots. "Charlie," she began on a deep breath as they crossed an intersection. "Fran and Joe are getting married."

Unmindful of oncoming traffic and the blare of a car horn, he stopped dead in his tracks, staring at her. "Really?"

"Really." She tugged him across the street by the sleeve. "And they're very happy about it. They're good together, Charlie. Even you know that."

He did. Fran and Joe were perfect for each other. He had thought so right from the beginning. And yet he couldn't help but add a satiric footnote. *Yeah sure, they're good together now, but just wait.* Marriage had a way of changing things. But then he reminded himself that not everybody had a union like his parents. In fact, nobody had a union like his parents, thank God. Some people managed to muddle along very well together for years and years. Still, the whole concept of spending fifty years with one person made his blood run cold. But then, even that thought was becoming easier and easier. Life was suddenly very complicated.

"Oh, by the way," Cassie added, taking another deep breath and deciding to give him the news all at once, "they want you to be the best man."

"Oh, no," Charlie groaned. "Not another monkey suit."

"The things we do for love," Cassie commiserated, hiding a smile.

They crossed into the heart of SoHo, where the once bohemian mecca had taken on the air of gentrification. "Why is it, Armstrong, that everything always has to change?" Charlie asked wistfully. It seemed an odd question for a man who thrived on change, but then Charlie was only good at changes he'd initiated, and he liked life just the way it was right now. "Fran and Joe. This neighborhood." Clear disdain written on his face, he eyed an upscale gourmet beanery. "I remember the days when coffee shop meant coffee shop."

Cassie flicked a glance at his ripped jeans, boat shoes and the inevitable T-shirt, and a laugh escaped her in spite of the seriousness of their conversation. "Don't worry, Charlie," she commented dryly. "Nobody will ever mistake you for a yuppie."

He swung around to stare at her. "What is this, Armstrong?" he demanded laughingly. "A trace of irony? A scintilla of dry wit? You know, I think I'm making progress corrupting you. You really are turning into a sophisticated, hardened New York type." Without warning, he swept her up in his arms, city street or no city street.

Cassie didn't even blush. "I think you're right," she agreed slowly as she stared into the eyes of the man she loved. "I've decided to live with you, Charlie Whitman."

The teasing left his face, leaving only the smile, a little uncertain now. Though he'd hoped, prayed, he'd never been certain that she'd actually go through with it. "Really?"

"Really."

Even as his heart surged with happiness, he resisted the urge to kiss her serious face for one more moment. "You won't be sorry," he told her, and it was both a promise and a vow.

When she was with Charlie she never doubted for one instant. It was only later that she prayed he was right and Fran was not.

THE ONLY THING LEFT to be decided was where they would live. Long into the night, they debated her place versus his.

"I am not the uptown type, Armstrong," he told her as they got ready for bed.

"My place is bigger," she pointed out logically. "Not to mention—" She flicked a glance at Charlie's haphazard piling system, the socks spilling out of his drawers, the books that never seemed to get back on the shelf. Although he was improving, improvement was a relative thing. "Neater."

"Clutter is a sign of genius, Armstrong."

"Well, then, Einstein move over, Charlie Whitman is in town."

He playfully fired a pillow at her head, laughing when she fired back. "Now about this apartment thing, Armstrong. How about if we draw straws for it? A game of pool perhaps? I know," he told her with a grin, "we could arm wrestle. But you'd probably win."

She fired another pillow, which he promptly shot back in retaliation.

"There you go again, Armstrong. Beating me up. What an Amazon."

Amazon or no, Cassie was adamant. If she could take a bold step and live with him, then he had to meet her at least halfway. He had to make some compromises, prove he was as committed to this relationship as she was.

"My place or the deal's off," she informed him, lobbing a pillow right at his head.

He was out of ammunition, both in pillows and in arguments. "Okay, okay," he agreed with an exaggerated sigh. "You win. Uptown it is. But if you so much as catch me glancing into a Brooks Brothers window, if I start developing a hankering for Brie, then the deal is off and we move down here."

Having seen Charlie's wardrobe and the contents of his refrigerator, she didn't think there was much danger there.

Cassie probably wouldn't have been surprised to learn that, instead of giving up his apartment, Charlie sublet it. *Just in case,* he told himself. But he didn't tell her. As usual, Charlie always held a part of himself back.

FOR TWO PEOPLE as different as they were, they lived together with surprising ease. Compromise proved the order of the day. Cassie learned to ease up on her need for organization, and Charlie attempted to pick up after himself. It helped that they were both wildly in love.

For Charlie it was the closest he'd ever come to a commitment to another person, but he no longer found it such a scary thing. In fact, he started to rely on it, to savor the fact that she'd be there when he got home, that there was another person with whom to share a good day or a bad one. He realized just how far he'd come when Cassie returned late one evening after a rough session with Vince.

Throwing her briefcase on the foyer table, she was soothed only by Charlie's kiss.

"Problems?" he asked, massaging her neck.

"This would be a great business," she told him as he steered her to the couch, "if it weren't for the clients."

Some of the tension started to leave her shoulders under the hypnotic ministrations of his fingers. "Sorry to dump on you," she told him with a sigh.

"Hey, that's what I'm here for," he reminded her as he leaned in for a kiss. Wanting her to forget, willing her to forget, he deepened the kiss until her head spun. "Feeling better?" he asked when they finally broke apart.

Dazed, Cassie smiled at him. "What client?" she murmured. "What problems?" She was only half joking.

With a small laugh, he helped her from the sofa. "How about some dinner? Maybe a little wine. You'll feel like a new woman."

Hand in hand, they wandered toward the dining alcove. Cassie's eyes widened to see that Charlie had set the table, had even included candles. A delicious aroma wafted from the kitchen, and she sniffed appreciatively. "You really are a wonder, Charlie Whitman. You cooked and everything."

"Oh, yeah, I can call for takeout with the best of them."

As they relaxed over a second glass of wine, Charlie brought up the subject of the agency once more. "About

Vince, Cassie. Why don't you just quit? Go back to school. You always said you wanted to teach. Well, here's your chance."

She sighed. "Nice dream. But how am I going to pay all my expenses, never mind the tuition?"

He hesitated only a beat. "How about me?"

Startled, she looked across the table at him. This was the first time he'd ever mentioned anything remotely resembling a long-term commitment. The first time he'd hinted at a lasting future together. As Cassie knew only too well, Charlie lived in the here and now. She was too surprised to know what to say.

Seeing her shock, he made a little of joke of it as he rose to clear the table. "What's the matter, Armstrong? Don't you think I can support you in the manner to which you've become unaccustomed?"

Following him, she placed a hand on his arm, stopping him by the sink. "Thanks for the offer, Charlie. I love you for that. You just surprised me, that's all. But then—" she smiled into those gray eyes "—you always surprise me. I suppose I love you for that, too."

"Feeling's mutual, Armstrong." He wrapped his arms around her waist, holding her against his body. "Think about it, okay?"

Serious blue eyes stared at him. She wanted Charlie to be sure. "Maybe we should both think about it."

But as his lips claimed hers, neither thought of the future anymore that night. The present was all too satisfying.

12

FRAN AND JOE'S wedding day dawned crisp and clear. There was not a cloud in the sky on that November morning, and not a doubt in anyone's heart, except maybe Charlie's. He grumbled about being stuffed into a monkey suit, but that was the least of his problems. He was going to meet Cassie's parents for the first time that day. Fran, as an honorary adopted member of the Armstrong clan, had invited all the Armstrongs to share her happiness, and Charlie was uncharacteristically nervous at the thought. Having never gotten quite so far along in a relationship before, he was a novice at this meet-the-parents stuff. Not to mention that he wasn't very good around families in the first place, particularly not happy families.

"Suppose they don't like me?" he asked Cassie, tying his cravat for the third time.

"Of course they'll like you." She pushed his hands aside to tie the cravat herself. "Who doesn't like you? Everyone always likes you."

True enough, but then he didn't live with anyone else's daughter without benefit of matrimony. He imagined the senior Armstrongs would be a fairly conservative couple, and he just prayed they could be as open-minded as their daughter.

Good daughter that she was, Cassie tried to pave the way in that regard. Over the phone, her parents on two different extensions, she'd explained her new living arrangement. "Mom, Dad," she began tentatively. "About Charlie . . ." There was no way to say it except say it. She was a full-grown woman, after all. She and her parents shared a loving relationship. They trusted her, valued her judgment, and even if they didn't wholeheartedly agree, what could they do?

"We can't wait to meet him, honey," her mother interjected into the silence.

"Yeah, sweetheart. Can't wait," her father echoed.

Somehow their kindness only made things worse. Florence and Frank Armstrong were not ogres, far from it. Still, they were not exactly jet-setters, either. Of her mother, she had fewer doubts. The quieter of the two, Florence tended to be less protective of the children than her father. Cassie thought about Frank Armstrong. A teller of jokes that only he found funny, Frank tended to guard his children, especially his daughters, like the old-fashioned fathers of rerun sitcoms. Still, her dad usually listened to his more down-to-earth wife in domestic matters. It was a family joke that her father only appeared to rule the household, when it was really the quiet Florence whose word was law, a fact only Frank seemed blissfully ignorant of.

"Yes, well, Mom and Dad, I think you'll really like Charlie, but . . . There is one small thing." She swallowed hard. "Charlie and I are living together."

She breathed a sigh of relief. It was out in the open now. It was to her parents' credit that she told them the truth. After all, she didn't have to. But it had never occurred to her to lie to them; that wasn't the way she was raised. She just hoped they'd see it that way.

On the other end, silence reigned. Though clearly as surprised as her husband, it was Florence who recovered first. "Oh, well, honey, that's . . ." Words clearly failed her. "Well, you know, it's a different world out there than when your father and I were dating. More . . ." She groped for an adjective. "More modern. Isn't that right, Frank?"

Her father cleared his throat. "Yeah, well, modern, sure. Not that modern is always good, mind you."

Not liking the direction her father was taking, Cassie sought to head him off at the pass. "Mom, Dad, I love Charlie and he loves me. And we're very happy together. I want you to be happy for me, okay?"

That was obviously enough for her mother. "We trust you, Cassie," she said quietly across the miles. "And if you love him, then we do, too."

"Thank you, Mom. I love you." That still left another party to be heard from.

"Cassandra Elaine Armstrong, I hope you know what you're—"

Her mother's firm voice stopped her father from gathering momentum. "Say good-night, Frank."

Frank Armstrong sighed. "My better half speaks. So before I get into any more trouble . . . Good night, Frank."

They all hung up the phone to the sound of laughter.

STILL, Cassie held her breath as she introduced Charlie to her large, exuberant family. Since Fran and Joe's wedding was to be held at the bride's Westchester home, Fran's dire predictions of bad luck aside, the assembled Armstrongs met at a nearby hotel and congregated in Cassie's room. Charlie had taken a separate room, albeit unwillingly. The small hotel room bulged with Cassie's assembled relatives—parents, brothers, sister and all their respective spouses, sons and daughters. And while Cassie was swallowed up in bear hugs and teary-eyed welcomes, Charlie stood apart.

He was grateful for the reprieve. It gave him a chance to get his bearings, a chance to look them over in private. It was impossible not to like this family. In Frank Armstrong, he saw Cassie's sense of humor and big blue eyes; in Florence, he read Cassie's quiet strength. Unlike his own parents, the elder Armstrongs seemed to complement each other. They were down-to-earth, yet spontaneous in their affection. Besides loving one another, they all seemed to honestly like one another, as well, an emotion that couldn't be faked, as Charlie knew only too well.

At long last, Cassie drew back, mindful of Charlie's presence. Given his own family, she wondered what this must be like for him. Wrapping her arm around his waist, she pulled him into the fray. "Mom and Dad, this is Charlie. Charlie, these are my parents, Florence and Frank Armstrong."

Florence stepped forward first. "So you're the young man we've been hearing so much about." Her smile matched her daughter's—quiet, welcoming, and instead of shaking his hand, she stood on tiptoe to kiss him gently on the cheek. "Welcome," she said softly. "I hope you don't mind," she apologized. "It's just we feel we know you already. Cassie's talked so much about you."

Charlie didn't mind at all. If anything, he was touched by the gesture. And the witticism he'd carefully prepared, about how she looked too young to be the mother of five children, died unsaid in his throat. Instead he merely replied, "Thank you. I feel like I know you already, too."

Frank Armstrong stepped forward and seized Charlie's hand in a firm grip. Perhaps a shade too firm, as he stared at the younger man, sizing him up. Charlie could hardly blame him for the scrutiny and bore it well, trying to look both sincere and mature, traits that didn't come easily. It appeared that he'd passed muster when Frank said, at last, "Good to meet you, son, as long as we don't have to kiss."

"I promise," Charlie told him as everyone laughed.

And then came a swarm of faces and names until Charlie groaned. "Just how many of you are there?"

"There'll be a short quiz later," Frank informed him, and Charlie sensed he was only half teasing, and that the quiz was not going to be about family names.

"You did great," Cassie whispered in his ear.

All too soon, the reunion ended and it was time for the wedding. In a little room in the back of the church, Cassie could only stare at the sight of her friend in her wedding gown, even though she'd helped pick it out. Gone was the sleek, cynical yuppie of the hot-pink minidresses and lime green pantsuits. In her stead was a vision in white, but it was Fran's expression that proved the most changed. Pure happiness and a tinge of panic shone in those once worldly eyes.

Her eyes swimming with tears, Cassie said, "Oh, Fran. You look so beautiful."

Glancing at the long, tiered dress, Fran nervously pleated a fold, then tinkered with her veil, displaying classic prewedding jitters. "Oh, God, what am I doing? I should have eloped. I mean, look at me. I don't even recognize myself." Panicky, she looked at Cassie. "You don't think it's too much, do you? People aren't going to laugh, are they?"

In answer, Cassie whirled Fran around to look at herself in the full-length mirror. Hands on her friend's shoulders, she demanded, "What do you think, Fran Gorham? Soon to be Fran Gorham Mancini."

The two friends' eyes met in the mirror. "I think we've come a long way," Fran said slowly.

They certainly had. "Grady Harriman, eat your heart out," Cassie said with a laugh, making Fran laugh, too.

"Cassie." Her friend's tone sobered. "Whatever I said about Charlie . . ."

"It's forgotten," Cassie assured her. And then it was too late to say any more. A knock sounded on the door. "Good luck," Cassie whispered.

Fran and Joe seemed to have made their own luck as they were united as husband and wife. The cynical Fran Gorham ceased to exist as Fran and Joe Mancini were showered with buckets of rice and choruses of congratulations.

Later on, during the country-club reception, the band broke into a familiar song. As the first strains of "You Made Me Love You" drifted through the room, Charlie sought Cassie out. "Excuse me," he informed the crowd gathered around her, "but I believe this is our song. I hope you don't mind if I borrow my date."

No one seemed to mind in the least. As Charlie led her out onto the crowded dance floor, several pairs of eyes beamed after them.

Cassie didn't notice anyone else. Her steps meshed perfectly with his. He returned her smile. "Have I told you you look beautiful today, Ms. Armstrong?"

She pretended to think it over. "Only a few dozen times. But not in the last five minutes."

Charlie grinned. She did look beautiful in her simple teal gown. Preferring the understated, she and Fran had avoided the usual wedding-party frills. Tonight, Cassie made the gown and not the other way around. Or maybe it was the luminous glow of happiness that lit those blue eyes, caressed those pink cheeks. "Well," Charlie said, "let me rectify that oversight right now. You look gorgeous tonight."

She felt gorgeous. Proprietarily, she brushed off a spot of lint from his morning suit and gave him the once-over. "You don't look too bad yourself, Whitman. Tails suit you, you know."

Charlie groaned in response, then whirled her about. "I like your parents."

She smiled at him. "They like you, too. I know you were nervous about meeting them, Charlie, but they really do like you. My mother told me, and she doesn't lie any better than I do."

Charlie had to laugh. "Remember the night we met?"

"How could I ever forget?"

His eyes found hers. "It's true, you know. This song." His arms tightened about her waist, drawing her even nearer. "I love you," he whispered into her ear.

"I love you, too."

As they moved across the floor to the strains of their song, Cassie wondered if she'd ever be this happy again. She tried to capture all the details of this second, the rough feel of Charlie's jacket against her bare flesh, the warm security of his arms, the smile on her parents' faces as they waltzed past them. Surrounded by all the people she loved so much, in the arms of the man she loved so much, she wanted this evening, this perfect moment, to go on and on.

But like all good things, this, too, ended. The outside world intruded, and with it other people's expectations.

All too soon, at least for Charlie and Cassie, Fran's father cut in, his face florid with exertion and drink. "So," he boomed in his hearty, overly jovial, man-about-town way. "You two make quite the matchmakers. But it's later than you think, eh, Charlie?" Swaying slightly on his feet, he winked unevenly. "Soon I suppose we'll be dancing at your wedding. If I was a few years younger I'd give you a run for this one." He flirted with drunken ease, and leered at Cassie.

Neither Charlie nor Cassie knew what to say, but the spell between them was broken. Fortunately, before Mr. Gorham could do any further damage the band stopped playing. All eyes were on the bride and groom. Fran and Joe exchanged a long kiss, and the guests went wild. As the couple cut the wedding cake, Mr. Gorham disappeared into the crowd, to be spotted later flirting with one of the catering staff.

"He didn't mean anything, Charlie," Cassie told him in an undertone. "Fran's father can be . . . well, eccentric."

"No problem," Charlie assured her, but she knew he was bothered even as they mingled with the other guests.

When it was time for the bride to throw the bouquet Cassie reluctantly joined all the other single women in the room. Although she would have preferred not to, she wasn't given any choice in the matter. *Don't, Fran,* she silently prayed. *Please don't.*

But Fran Gorham Mancini had better sense than that. With a long glance in Cassie's direction, she deliberately tossed the bouquet of flowers toward the other side of the room. Cassie breathed a sigh of relief that proved a trifle premature. Her ten-year-old niece caught it and, with the unselfconsciousness of the very young, proudly presented it to her aunt as everyone looked on. "Here, Aunt Cassie." She beamed. "You and Uncle Charlie will need these before I will."

"Thank you, honey." Cassie managed to smile graciously, managed to accept the bouquet, but even as she did she looked everywhere but at "Uncle" Charlie.

Finally it was time to go home. "Come for the holidays, Charlie," her mother urged in the parking lot as the Armstrongs piled into cars and vans.

"Yeah," Frank Armstrong echoed, "you're one of the family now."

Everybody was trying to be nice, but the nicer they were, the harder it was. On the ride home, Charlie and Cassie were both quiet; she characteristically so, he uncharacteristically. It was not the companionable silence they normally shared these days.

As Charlie restlessly switched radio channels, Cassie broke the silence. "Charlie, I'm sorry."

His return smile was bland. "For what? Hey, it was a great evening. I had a wonderful time."

Charlie's defenses were up. "Charlie, I just want you to know I understand, okay? There's no pressure here. Not from me."

He was silent for a long time and then he looked at her. "I don't deserve you. You know that, don't you?"

Cassie found a smile. "I do know that."

He reached for her hand and squeezed it tightly. "Just be patient with me, Cassie, okay?" Through the darkness, his eyes held hers.

"Okay," she agreed with a more genuine smile, and hand in hand, they drove home.

13

THE HOLIDAYS LOOMED—Thanksgiving, then Christmas. Charlie had always hated this time of year. For him, the holidays had always spelled loneliness. He remembered waiting in prep school after prep school for missives from his parents that would decide his vacation fate. More often than not, the invitation to join them never came. More often than not, he found himself spending breaks with schoolmates' families, trying to pretend he fit in. Everybody had always been very nice, very kind, but in their pitying glances, the truth shone—he was the poor little kid with no place else to go.

As an adult, he fared better. Not that Sylvia and Charles had begun showering him with familial love. But as a grown-up, he could pretend that November slid into New Year's with no break in between. This year, however, was different. This year, he couldn't ignore the upcoming festive events. Cassie wouldn't let him.

"Charlie," she demanded early one Saturday morning late in November. "What about Thanksgiving? It's only a week away. Are you coming to my parents' or not?"

She hated the nagging tone in her voice, hated that he made her nag him, but there was no other way to rouse a response from him these days. She loved

Christmas, wanted to share her joy with the man she loved. But Charlie refused to cooperate, refused to make one single plan. Worse yet, she didn't think she'd seen him so much as smile in weeks.

Stretched out on the sofa, he buried his nose deeper in the newspaper. "I don't know," he muttered vaguely. "I'll see." But she refused to go away. Sighing, he stabbed her with a glance. "Do we have to talk about this now?"

"Well, when do you think would be a good time for you? I've been asking you for weeks."

"I'll let you know, all right?"

It wasn't all right. "Why don't you at least come Christmas shopping with me, Charlie?" *Do something, do anything,* she thought. *At least pretend you're alive.*

"I don't feel like it."

"You don't feel like doing anything anymore." The words burst out of her, that patience she'd promised him wearing thin. "And what about Christmas?" she insisted. "Are you coming home with me then?"

He slammed the paper down. "You're not going to give up, are you? Why are you doing this? Why are you deliberately picking a fight?"

"I'm not. I'm not picking a fight. I just happen to love you, Charlie Whitman."

"And I love you, too. But—" He dragged a hand through his hair. "What do you want from me, Cassie? Do you want me to pretend this is my favorite time of year? Well, it just isn't, all right? I'm sorry, I can't walk around pretending to be merry when I don't feel merry. Now just leave it alone."

But she wouldn't, couldn't. Other than their first breakup, this was the closest they'd ever come to a fight. "Just ignoring the holidays will not make them go away, Charlie."

"Really. It's worked rather well in the past. Until now, that is."

She tried not to be hurt by his sarcasm. No, she thought. It hadn't worked at all. That's why they were having this argument now. Her patience snapped. She was not very good at fights. She kept waiting for Charlie to tear down the walls by himself, let her all the way in, but she knew that wasn't going to happen without a push from her. "Do you know what your problem is, Charlie Whitman?"

"No, but I'm sure you're going to tell me."

It was because she loved him that she said what she did. It was something she'd thought now for a long, long time, but she'd always held back, afraid to say it aloud, afraid to hurt him. But she was finding out that you had to risk hurting the people you loved the most. "You're still letting your parents control your life, Charlie. Inside, you're still that little eight-year-old child. Charlie, you're letting them win."

It hit him like a blow, worse than a blow. Direct hit. Bull's-eye. Charlie Whitman's carefully concealed identity lay bared to the world. That it was the truth, that she clearly hadn't intended those words to hurt him, only made it worse. In its aftermath he wasn't sure which bothered him most, that she had said it at all or that she was getting too close.

She seemed to sense it, as well, for she left the apartment then. "Think about it, Charlie," was all she said.

As if he could do anything else. *Right*, Charlie thought, *call me an emotional cripple and then leave to Christmas shop. No guts, Armstrong.* "So what are you, a shrink all of a sudden?" he yelled after her. "I should have known you'd turn on me, too." But she was already gone. Hanging his head in his hands, he wondered when he had forgotten the simple lesson hurt first, or be hurt. No matter what he did, it was never good enough. What did she want from him, damn it? He knew what *she* wanted. She wanted him to let go of the past completely, let down all the barriers, let her all the way in. Except he wasn't sure if he could do that—ever.

When Cassie returned empty-handed, she and Charlie circled each other warily. Hanging up her coat with exquisite care, she was all too aware of Charlie still plopped on the sofa and knew he was only pretending to watch television. Closing the closet door, she turned toward him, staring at the man she loved, that curly brown hair, those gray eyes, all Charlie Whitman was . . . and wasn't.

"Charlie, I'm sorry if I hurt you," she said finally.

He saw the misery on her face and started to melt, started toward her. He didn't like to fight either, never had, and especially not with her. Never with her.

"But—" she held him off, a hand on his chest, knowing she had to go on "—I'm not sorry I said it."

His hands fell to his sides. "I see."

No further words were exchanged. She didn't mention the holidays again, and neither did he. On the surface they went on as before, but everything was changed. Everything was different. The closeness between them had turned to tension.

He supposed that was why, when the phone call came, he listened. It hit him at exactly the wrong moment, exactly when he felt the most vulnerable and therefore the most trapped.

"Hey, buddy," a voice greeted him cheerfully on the other end of the receiver. "How's it hangin', guy?"

"Rick!" Charlie exclaimed. "Rick Morissey, is that really you? Talk about a blast from the past. But how did you find me?" Or more specifically, how did he find him at Cassie's apartment?

"It wasn't easy, big guy. I had to call in just about every marker. So, where you hiding yourself?"

"It's a long story," Charlie told him. Rick Morissey was the closest thing to a best friend Charlie had. Not that they'd shared any intimate confidences, but Rick was a true hang-out buddy in the best and worst sense of that term. Together by night, they'd chased women, hit all the high spots New York had to offer, then churned out award-winning copy by day while nursing hangovers. A kindred spirit, Rick had kicked around as much if not more than Charlie. Twice divorced and into a shaky third marriage, his friend had abruptly left the New York agency scene one day to open up his own shop in Southern California. Though the two men talked once in a while, it wasn't the same, and Charlie had missed him. It was with true pleasure that Charlie greeted that long-lost voice. "Rick, I don't believe this. How the hell are you?"

"Perfect," his friend informed him with his usual breezy self-confidence. "I've still got my own agency. In fact, it's doin' great, too good, almost. That's why I'm calling you, big guy. I need a partner. A key man, so to speak. Somebody who understands the yins and yangs of this business, if you catch my drift. And, of course, buddy, right away, I thought of you."

"What?" Charlie laughed. "Rick, I think you've been in Moonbeam City too long. What are you talking about, man?"

But Rick seemed serious, if serious was a term that could ever be applied to the footloose and fancy-free. "I'm talking about a partnership, Charlie. You and me, together. Just like the old days. Only this time we'd be callin' our own shots. No uptight account types breathin' down our necks all day long. We'd be the big cheeses, runnin' the show."

Wrapping the phone cord around and around his hand, Charlie tried to clear his head. "You mean you want me to move to California?"

"You're about as sharp as a meatball today, Charlie," came the breezy response. "Of course, that's what I mean. It's seventy degrees out here, bud, and just like the song goes, it never rains in Southern California."

Parting the blinds with his free hand, Charlie glanced down onto Fifty-seventh Street. "It's gray and sleeting here."

"Good. So you'll come."

Dropping the blinds, Charlie paced the room. "Wait a minute! I can't just pack up and leave for California."

"Why not?"

Why not? That was a good question. Once upon a time and not too long ago, he would have been on the next plane out, no questions asked, but things were different now.

A test, Charlie thought. This was some kind of test. Like the serpent entering the Garden of Eden. He knew he should politely refuse, knew he should hang up the phone, but thinking of Cassie, the ongoing tension between them, the way they'd left things, made him hold on the line. "Hey, Rick, I'm flattered, man. But . . ." He paused. "I've got somebody . . ."

"You married?"

He heard the startled surprise in Rick's voice. So his best friend, the man who knew him better than anyone on this earth except maybe Cassie, couldn't imagine him married, either. "No, no," Charlie quickly assured him. "But . . . we're living together. She works at the same agency I do. In account management."

Rick whistled low in his throat. "I can't picture you settled down with any one woman, Charlie, and not somebody in account management. Well . . ." His voice trailed off, and then he seemed to recover, "Well, hell, bud, bring her along. I mean, I got so much work out here I could use another person."

Charlie tried to picture Cassie in Southern California, land of palm trees and glitz. The vision refused to come. It was not Cassie's style at all, never mind the fact that it was three thousand miles away from her parents. He wasn't even sure if he was interested in the job. Sure, it promised big bucks and a piece of the action, but it also promised high pressure and stress. And though he loved the creative product, administration was not his thing at all. Still, this opportunity provided him with an out. The fact that he felt he needed an alternative right about now proved just how much the holidays, and Cassie's attitude toward them, had unnerved him. "I'll think about it," he said finally.

"Do that, buddy. But think fast, all right? Not that you ever do things any other way. I need you, big guy. Listen, I'll call in a few weeks, okay?"

"Okay," Charlie heard himself agree.

IF CHARLIE MADE his first big mistake when he listened to the offer, he made his second when he didn't tell Cassie about it. But why tell her? Why upset her about something that would probably never happen anyway? Rick would probably forget all about him in his usual lackadaisical style, and Charlie wasn't sure he even wanted the job. Not to mention that he was angry with Cassie.

The problem was, it was difficult to stay angry at a woman who had only spoken the truth in the first place, and only had his best interests at heart. Charlie might be blind but he wasn't entirely stupid. And so, on Thanksgiving morning, with no nagging on her part, he found himself rising out of bed and donning a suit and a tie.

Snapping on earrings, Cassie caught his reflection in the mirror. "What are you doing?"

"Getting dressed for Thanksgiving dinner at your parents'." He hesitated. "That is, if I'm still invited?"

"Oh, Charlie." She ran into his arms.

He kissed her hard, hungrily, sweeping his hands through her thick hair. He'd missed this, missed her. Just how much, he realized only then.

Breathless, she pulled back a step. "Charlie, I hope you're not doing this because you feel pressured...."

Her earnestness had always moved him, even when he hadn't wanted it to. It moved him now. "Armstrong," he murmured against her lips, "no offense, but you talk too much." Scooping her up in his arms, he carried her the few feet to the bed, placing her gently on the mattress, so gently her heart caught.

She toyed with the buttons of his shirt. "And here we just got dressed."

"And you're also far too organized." Catching her hand, he grazed the knuckles with a kiss, then rested her hand on his cheek.

Looking at him, Cassie saw something in his expression that made her catch her breath.

Charlie's hand slid lower. Moving with infinite care and tantalizing slowness, he eased open the buttons of her silk dress, kissed the creamy flesh he bared, loving the way she sighed at him, opened to him until no barriers remained between them...not even the ones in his mind.

"Charlie," she moaned.

Whatever he asked of her, she gave, but then Cassie always gave. It was he who was different this time.

Tender, gentle, he scarcely recognized himself, and yet, in a funny way, he did, realizing that he'd always had the capacity to be tender and gentle, only it had been buried that day he was eight years old. He was rediscovering that part of himself.

He made love to her not just with his body, but also with his heart.

Cassie felt the difference, too. Even at the moment of their mutual triumph, she found and held those gray eyes. "I love you, Charlie Whitman."

"And I love you."

ON THE CAR RIDE to Kingston, they talked.

"Charlie, about Christmas," she began.

She'd thought long and hard about this, but if Charlie could compromise, then so could she. She didn't want to miss Christmas morning, when her entire family sat around in their bathrobes ripping open presents until the living room floor was buried under mounds of glittery paper. She had never missed one, not in her entire thirty years. But she also knew that Charlie's remembrances of holidays past were far from pleasurable. She had to put herself in his shoes and realize how painful it would be for him to be in the midst of her large, exuberant family while his remained lost to him. They had not heard a word from the senior Whitmans since that day in Connecticut. She feared they never would. Sylvia did not seem the type to back down, and Charlie certainly never would, not after what Sylvia said. Cassie supposed she was his only family now. "I just want you to know I understand. How about if I spend Christmas Eve with them and then Christmas Day with you?"

Ignoring the traffic for a minute, Charlie found her eyes. "Would you really do that for me?"

She didn't even have to think about her answer. "Yes."

"Well, I don't know," he murmured. "Christmas with your family might be fun." He reached for her hand. "After all, I'd be with you."

As their fingers joined, all their problems seemed behind them.

RETURNING TO THE CITY on Saturday morning, sated from too much turkey and replete with Armstrong family warmth, they plopped down on the sofa. Once they'd unpacked, Cassie suggested they go pick out a Christmas tree. "It's an Armstrong family tradition," she informed him. "We always put up the tree right after Thanksgiving."

Too lazy to move, Charlie resisted. "Well, it's not a Whitman one." As far as he knew they didn't have any family traditions save fighting to the death, which was all the more reason to bow to Cassie's desires, he supposed. Besides, he couldn't resist the little-girl excitement written all over her face.

Later, as they dragged the stupid thing up to the fourteenth floor, he had second thoughts. "An eight-foot tree," he huffed as he waited for her to open the door. "Don't you think this is overkill, Armstrong? I mean, our apartment isn't even this big."

Refusing to have her happiness diminished, she swiped a kiss across his disgruntled lips. "Just wait until you see this thing decorated. You won't be sorry then. Of course, we'll need to buy a lot of ornaments this year."

He cast her a terrified look. "We're not going to do that today, are we?"

"Of course not." She smiled. "Tomorrow."

Charlie rolled his eyes. "Christmas, bah, humbug. Now where do you want this monstrosity, Armstrong?"

With a thoughtful glance around the apartment, she gestured toward the bay window. "Right there. Perfect."

"Of course, Armstrong. On the far side of the room. No problem."

As he grappled with the tree, she grinned, then started toward the answering machine. "Have you played this thing back yet?" she called out.

When Charlie merely grunted in response, she hit play.

Though Cassie didn't know it then, Rick's breezy voice greeted her. "Hey, buddy. It's seventy-five degrees in sunny California and—"

Dropping the tree in the middle of the living room floor, Charlie lunged for the off button just in time. Or maybe not. He caught Cassie's stare. "Listen, would you mind giving me a hand with this thing? It's the least you can do since you picked a tree suitable for Rockefeller Center."

His tone was light. His eyes weren't. He looked, she thought, guilty. "Who was that, Charlie?"

He shrugged. "Nobody. Just a friend of mine. Now about this tree . . ."

The diversion didn't work. Charlie's guilty gray eyes met Cassie's determined blue ones.

Running a hand through his hair, he started to pace, but he knew if he didn't tell her, she'd find out anyway. Better to come clean now. Still, he couldn't quite seem to find the words.

"What's going on, Charlie?" she asked quietly.

"It's just some guy calling from California. An old buddy of mine. He owns his own agency and he offered me a job." Charlie hesitated only a beat before he added, "Of course, I told him no. That's it. End of story, okay? Now, can we get back to this tree?"

Cassie held her ground. "Then why didn't you tell me, Charlie?"

"Because there's nothing to tell, that's why."

"Then why," Cassie asked logically, "is he calling you back?"

"How should I know?" he burst out, trying not to sound defensive and knowing he did. "He's a persistent kind of guy."

"Or maybe," Cassie suggested, "you didn't tell him no."

The statement hung in the air between them, and when Charlie didn't deny it right away, she knew she was right. The only problem was, she didn't want to be right. Not now. Not about this. But she made herself go on. "Maybe you really want to go to California. Maybe you really want out of this relationship. Maybe this is all just a convenient excuse."

"No!" The denial tore out of him. "It isn't like that." He started to pace the room, back and forth, to and fro. "I admit I didn't exactly tell him no. But I didn't tell him yes, either. And if you'll recall, we were fighting at the time. We—"

She wouldn't let him finish. "So what, Charlie? What does that mean? That every time we have a fight, you'll take off? I'll get a postcard from you?"

"Hey, I'm still here, aren't I? And I wasn't planning on just taking off. I asked about a job for you, too."

That scarcely mollified her. "Without consulting me? You just decided?"

"I wasn't thinking straight. Look." He ran a hand through his hair. "I admit it. I was wrong. And I'm sorry. But you're twisting this whole thing out of proportion."

She didn't think so. This was Charlie's classic pattern, wasn't it? Running away. Unbidden, Fran's words came to her. Fran's cynicism had been right on target, at least about Charlie Whitman. *People don't change*, she heard her friend say as if she was in the room. Charlie hadn't changed at all, but then neither had she, really. No matter where she lived, no matter who she was with, she would always be that small-town girl, slightly naive, who believed in family and commitments, in till death do us part and happily ever after.

She'd always thought, up until this moment, that she'd have those things with Charlie, but now, right now, doubt crept in.

Her entire life hung in the balance. She knew that as surely as she knew her name. The timing seemed so incongruous, right before the holidays, their first Christmas tree, that symbol of hope, lying, forgotten, on its side. She forced herself to meet his eyes. Forced herself to take a deep breath. "Let's say we take these jobs, Charlie. Move to California. Then what?"

"I don't know what you mean. And I never said I wanted to go to California."

"So what do we do then? Keep playing house? Keep moving to the next job, the next town?"

"Well, what are you looking for? Some kind of lifetime guarantee?"

"Yeah, Charlie." She met and held his eyes, forcing him to look at her, really look at her and see her for what she was, and what he was, as well. "I suppose that's exactly what I'm looking for."

"Oh, so what do you want to do?" he demanded. "Get married? Is that what this is all about?"

And that's when her heart broke. It was something she'd always read about, seen in movies. She had never believed it could happen in real life. Now she knew differently. For in that moment, she knew the truth. Charlie Whitman loved her, and she loved him, but Fran was right. He loved her as much as he was able, he loved her as much as he could, but he wouldn't, couldn't love her the way she deserved to be loved. And in that instant, she also recognized the truth about herself. If Charlie was a product of his environment, then so was she. She didn't want to live her life in the fast lane. She didn't want to work in advertising anymore. She wanted to go back to school, she wanted to teach, and she wanted a little house somewhere with roses she could carefully and lovingly cultivate each year. And she wanted a family. She wanted to be part of a family. She wanted these things with Charlie because she loved him. She'd always believed, always allowed herself to believe, up until that moment, that Charlie would come to his senses. Wake up. Grow up. Now she knew differently. Charlie couldn't change any more than she could. She was never going to get the things she wanted with Charlie Whitman. Not now. Not ever.

And even as Charlie had said those hateful words, he'd known he was wrong. "God, I'm sorry. Look, I didn't mean that. Of course, we'll get married."

Maybe he really would marry her, Cassie thought. But how long until he felt trapped? How long until he grew restless, wanted out? No. It was over, and the sooner the better for both of them.

"No, Charlie," she heard herself say. "I think you should go to California. Alone."

"What? What are you saying? What do you mean?" He stared at her, confused and suddenly afraid. "Are you breaking up with me?"

She was, wasn't she? The impact of what she was doing hit her like a physical blow. But deep down where it counted, Cassie was tougher than he was. "That's exactly what I'm saying, Charlie. I'd appreciate it if you'd move out as soon as possible."

"But why? Look, this is crazy. We love each other. I just asked you to marry me."

She couldn't listen anymore, afraid he just might change her mind. She had to get away. "Look, stay here tonight," she told him. "I'll go to Fran and Joe's." She made a phone call, threw a few things into a bag and was gone.

IN THE DAYS that followed, he pleaded, he cajoled, he even begged, but all to no avail. It was as if Cassie Armstrong had turned to stone. Stubbornly, he refused to move out, refused to give up. And one week later, he came to her with a small jewelry box. With shaky knees and an even more quivery voice, he presented it to her. "Please, Cassie. Please marry me. I love you."

Her heart broke a second time. The solitaire diamond seemed to wink at her, promising all that could be. She turned her head away. "Charlie, if you love me, if you really love me, then go away."

With nowhere left to turn, Charlie packed his bags for California. Even before the plane touched down, he knew he was making the biggest mistake of his life.

Alone in New York, Cassie stared at the now empty apartment. Devoid of all Charlie's clutter, the place seemed bigger somehow. And that's when she finally cried.

14

HE SHOULD HAVE loved Los Angeles. Fast moving, slick, it was everything Charlie Whitman had once been. He hated it. He hated every palm tree, he hated the invariable beautiful weather, he hated the golden-haired bathing beauties with their available smiles, and most of all, he hated his job. He hated the endless management decisions, the interminable meetings. He hated writing copy for stupid things people didn't need in the first place and couldn't afford even if they did. As he'd once claimed, advertising wasn't brain surgery, and for the first time that bothered him. His career had turned on him.

Mostly, he felt lonely, afraid and confused. He felt like a pitiful eight-year-old child. Except this time was even worse. This time, he'd had control. Holding happiness in his two hands, he had thrown it away. Of course, he wanted to marry her. How could he ever have doubted that? He couldn't imagine a lifetime without her at his side. The next fifty years of freedom stretched ahead, lonely and bleak.

In desperation, he turned to his manuscript. Like everything else in his life, it was started but not finished, showed raw potential, but no real substance. Then again, what did he know about commitments? He'd spent a lifetime avoiding the topic.

But not this time. This time Charlie Whitman had come to the end of the line.

Hunched over the typewriter, he wrote and rewrote, tried a little harder, dug deeper. And within those rapidly growing pages, he caught a glimmer of the man he could be.

The other thing that kept him going was his conversations with Fran, the only contact he had with Cassie. The chapters of his book flowed, if not his chats with Cassie's best friend.

"Fran," he pleaded. "Please, please don't hang up."

"I should, you know. You swine. You pig."

He offered little in his own defense. "How is she, Fran?"

"She's fine." That was not exactly the truth. Cassie went about the business of living, she dutifully reported to the agency each day and she'd even sent out applications for graduate school, but she was so pale, Fran was afraid for her. Cassie Armstrong looked like the ghost of Christmas past.

"Take care of her for me, Fran, okay?"

"For you?" Fran's strident tone cut through the three thousand miles that separated them. "You've got a hell of a lot of nerve, Charlie."

Gently, he replaced the phone in its cradle and returned to his typewriter.

HE CALLED AGAIN on Christmas Day. "Is she okay, Fran?" he asked without preamble.

Cassie was spending the week with her family, and when Fran had talked to her yesterday, the truth was she had sounded better than Charlie did. Even across the miles, he seemed tense, strung out. "Are you?" Fran asked, against her better judgment. "You sound a little strange."

He felt a little strange. Almost as if he'd given birth, and in a way he supposed he had. "Oh, well, I've been writing. A novel . . . about commitments."

Fran almost dropped the line. "What? I think we must have a bad connection, Charlie. I thought you just said you were writing a novel . . . about commitments."

"I am. In fact, it's done. I've sent it to an agent in New York and he seems interested and . . ." He paused. "I'd like you to read it, too."

Covering the receiver with one hand, she turned to Joe. "It's Charlie," she whispered. "He sounds kind of funny and he says he's written a novel, about commitments, of all things. He wants me to read it. What should I do?"

Joe merely shrugged.

"Right," Fran answered, reading her husband's eloquent silence. "Just like you men to stick together." Hoping she was doing the right thing and feeling guilty, as if she was consorting with the enemy, she replied, "Fine. Send it out."

Shortly after, a parcel arrived at Fran and Joe's New York apartment. Tearing open the brown paper, she devoured the contents. By the time she'd finished, tears swam in her eyes. Ignoring Joe's questioning glance, she grabbed up the manuscript and flew out of the apartment to Cassie's place.

Her friend had barely opened the door when Fran thrust it under her nose. "Here. Read it. It's a novel. Charlie has written a novel. About you. I mean, about you and him. And wait until you read the ending. It's unbelievable. I don't believe it."

Cassie stared at her. "I didn't know you were talking to Charlie."

"I haven't. Not really. Well, maybe a couple of times." With an impatient breath, she pushed the typed pages into Cassie's hands. "Look, just read it, and then you can be mad at me later."

The dedication page alone made Cassie catch her breath. "To Cassie," she read. "Forever and always. Believe me." Weakly, she sank into an upholstered chair, her eyes skittering to Fran's.

"Read the rest," Fran encouraged, but Cassie couldn't seem to focus, couldn't seem to take it all in.

"You read it," Cassie told her.

Clearing her voice, Fran began to read. "Chapter One. 'He spotted her first. Across the length of a packed hotel ballroom, his eyes restlessly scanned the crowd, then doubled back, locked on the figure of a woman in a simple red dress. She had thick, shoulder-length hair the color of taffy and blue, blue eyes, so blue a man could lose himself in them. And though he didn't even know her name, he knew his life had changed forever.'" Fran paused then, glancing up. "I can't take it anymore. Do you want to know how it ends?" Without waiting for an answer she rushed on, "They get married and everything. It's unbelievable, Cassie. He's changed. He's really changed. And he's coming to New York to see you! At least, if you want to see him." She looked at Cassie to see how she was taking this, but Cassie just sat there. "Cassie, have you heard a word I've said?" Unable to contain her excitement, Fran flipped to the back. "Let me just read you the end. That'll convince you."

But Cassie's voice stopped her. "Charlie doesn't know how it ends," she told her friend.

Her enigmatic smile made Fran pause. Confused, she stared. "Cassie, what do you mean? Unless . . . What are you saying? That you don't want to see him? Honey, look, I'll admit I'm the last person on earth to believe Charlie Whitman could ever change. But, Cassie, he has."

That Mona Lisa smile flashed again. "Charlie Whitman isn't the only one who's changed."

"Why do I get the funny feeling," Fran asked slowly, "that I'm missing something here?"

There were some things Cassie couldn't tell even her best friend. Not yet. Not until she'd talked to Charlie first. "That's only the first installment of the book," Cassie told Fran by way of explanation. "Just wait until you hear the sequel."

15

FEELING LIKE a criminal returning to the scene of his crime, Charlie hovered on the threshold of what was once their Upper East Side apartment. Living together, he thought, the ultimate commitment of the uncommitted. Together, not in a state of grace, but in a state of limbo; perfect for the man he used to be. But he was not that man anymore. That man had been blind, stupid and afraid. The new, improved Charlie Whitman planned to disprove all that today. He was going to ask Cassie—no, correction, beg her—to marry him. And he was going to be so mature, so sophisticated, so compelling and so cogent in his argument that refusal would be rendered impossible.

Her voice startled him.

"Are you planning on coming in, Charlie, or—" her voice held the merest hint of a smile "—is this it for the night?"

Confused, he glanced around, surprised to find himself still in the doorway. So much for maturity and sophistication, he thought, stepping inside. Perhaps he should resort to Plan B, pure begging. A less-suave approach, to be sure, but it was difficult to be suave when your knees knocked together and you could scarcely breathe. Each movement magnified in importance, he watched as she closed the door behind them, then turned to take his coat, her eyes widening slightly at the sight of his suit. He'd changed clothes three times before coming over here, and now he wasn't sure again. But he forgot all about what he wore when he risked a glance at her face. Having not seen her in a month, he couldn't help but stare, the gape of a dying man at the sight of salvation.

She looked good—wonderful, in fact. Just as he'd pictured her so often over the past few weeks. The same blue, blue eyes, the same mane of taffy-colored hair. Right from the moment he'd laid eyes on her, he'd wanted her. He wanted her now, wanted to sweep her up in his arms and carry her away into the night. And when she smiled slightly, a faint blush on her cheeks, he started to hurl the question at her—will you marry me? But he didn't. Newfound wisdom and maturity held him silent, made him cautious. He'd been reckless and heedless before and didn't plan to make the same mistake twice, except he couldn't think of a single thing to say. Just when he needed it most, his glibness deserted him, leaving him high and dry. He could only be himself, and being himself was what scared Charlie Whitman to death.

Fortunately, Cassie seemed to possess sufficient presence of mind for both of them. "We won an award, Charlie. Our campaign for Majik Toys won a CLEO."

"Oh, yeah." His eyes focused on hers. "I guess we do make a good team, huh?"

Though she smiled faintly, he couldn't read more into it than just a smile.

"So, how are you, Charlie?"

Miserable, lonely, confused, scared. Pick one of the above. "Okay. How are you?"

Squarely, those blue eyes met his own. "I've been better, to tell you the truth."

That small exchange summed up the difference between them. People thought of Cassie Armstrong as a soft touch, a pushover. Even he had made that mistake. But deep down, where it counted, Cassie was strong, stronger than he for all his bravado. It was she who'd had the integrity and the courage to walk away.

Cassie Armstrong wished for some of that courage right now. Although he might not know it, Charlie wasn't the only one in this room who was scared. She had a news flash of her own, a big one, only she wasn't entirely sure how he'd take it. Uncharacteristically, she stalled for time. "Have you talked to your parents, Charlie?"

He had. The contact had been initiated by them. Nominally it had been his father who called, but Charlie knew that the elderly man would never have done anything that wasn't Sylvia's idea. A face-saving device if ever he saw one, true, but at least she had tried. The conversation had been awkward, stilted, but there had been no unpleasantness. For them, that was good, or at least as good as could be expected. It seemed all the pieces of his life were falling into place, except maybe one, the one standing before him. "Yeah," Charlie said, not really thinking of his parents at all. "I talked to them." He even tried for a joke. "They're still together last I heard, but then it's been twenty minutes."

Charlie's humor always made her smile. She smiled now.

Seeing it, Charlie seized a little courage of his own. "So did you read it?"

She nodded. "Your book? Yes, I read it."

He knew she would. He knew Fran would make her read it. That's why he'd sent it to Fran in the first place. "And?"

He didn't realize so much could hang on one simple word, but his life hung in the balance.

"It's good, Charlie. It's very good."

That was not the answer he was looking for. Running a hand through his hair, he burst out, "I'm not asking for damned literary criticism, Cassie. The whole point of the book is— Oh hell!" He fought to regain control and found it at long length. He turned to face her then, squarely meeting her eyes. "Cassandra Elaine Armstrong, will you marry me?"

"Charlie, I—" *Yes*, she wanted to shout, but she couldn't. Not yet. Instead, she bit her lip. "Charlie, we need to talk."

He thought that's what they had been doing. Why was she so nervous? He wondered. Unless... Unless she planned to say no. But he had been so sure.... "Cassie, I've changed. I really have. I'm not afraid anymore. Well, yes, I am, but only of the thought of the next fifty years without you."

"I know you've changed, Charlie," she answered gently. "It's not that, but—" She bit her lip. "I've changed, too."

She didn't love him anymore. That was it. He had waited too long. "Cassie, look, give me another chance and I'll—"

"I'm pregnant, Charlie."

"—prove it to you, I'll—" He stopped and stared at her. "What?"

She hadn't meant to tell him like that, not so bluntly, but how could she ever ease him into an announcement like that?

Despite his question, she knew he'd heard her correctly as she watched the surprise spread into his eyes. Though she searched for some reaction beyond surprise, that's all she saw. She couldn't blame him. He was mirroring her feelings when she'd read the test vial, heard the doctor's voice. Shocked surprise and then elation. In one moment she'd thought her life was over and in the next she'd known it had only begun. She wanted Charlie to be happy about it, too.

The only thing harder than telling him once, she decided, was telling him twice, and she refused to do it. Instead, she defiantly met his eyes. She was happy about this baby, damn it, and she wasn't going to back down. Not now. Not ever. No matter what the consequences. "I think you heard me, Charlie Whitman."

She wore that ferocious look she'd had that night she'd decked him one, and he knew right then it was true. She really was pregnant. A thousand questions flooded his mind. What? Where? When? How?

Wordlessly, she seemed to read his thoughts. "We're both fine," she told him. "A textbook case, according to the doctor." She hesitated only a beat. "I'm eight weeks along."

Eight weeks, Charlie thought. That would make it... Thanksgiving. That magical time they'd made up. He'd known something was different that time, only he'd thought it was him. His eyes flashed to her, and she nodded slowly.

Suddenly, it hit him, really hit him. Oh, my God, he thought, almost hysterical in his relief. It was all right.

Everything was going to be all right. The weeks of tension and worry caught up with him, and suddenly he was laughing. Couldn't seem to stop laughing, couldn't seem to help himself.

Cassie could only stare at him. Whatever reaction she'd expected from this man, and she'd imagined dozens of scenarios, it wasn't that. She almost did deck him then, except, before she could, something hit her, too. Charlie Whitman looked happy. But then Charlie Whitman, right from the beginning, had always done the unpredictable. She supposed that's what she loved about him and always would.

16

WIPING A TEAR of laughter from his eye, Charlie caught Cassie's stare and managed to sober himself. "Don't you see, Armstrong?" he said with a grin. "This is perfect, better than perfect. Now you have to marry me."

Observing that grin, her heart started to take flight, but she postponed the moment. "And that makes you happy, Charlie Whitman, coercing me into marriage?"

"Damn straight. That makes me delirious. Because I just happen to be madly in love with you, the baby is—" he gestured with his hands as if couldn't find the words "—icing on the cake." He sobered and shot her a glance, a trace of uncertainty in it now. "You *are* going to marry me, aren't you?"

She pretended to think it over, but her grin gave her away. "I guess I'll have to. Because, you see, I just happen to be madly in love with you, too."

Suddenly, they were in each other's arms, neither sure who had moved first and neither caring very much as their lips met.

"Oops," Charlie said after a time. "There seems to be one last thing we forgot." From his coat pocket, he extracted the jewelry box he'd been carrying around for a month. Slipping the ring on her finger—a perfect fit— he met her eyes. "You can't get away from me this time, Armstrong. Now it's official."

Full circle, just like that band he had given her, it was Charlie Whitman who wanted a commitment now.

CASSIE ARGUED for a small, quiet ceremony, but having come this far, Charlie was adamant. "No way, Armstrong. After all, I'm only getting married once. I want to shoot the works on this one. I want to invite everyone we know and hold it in the ballroom where we met."

"But, Charlie, there isn't enough time to plan."

He silenced her worrying with a kiss, the magic between them powerful. In the end, no one was very surprised, least of all Cassie herself, when Charlie Whitman got his wish. By calling in every favor owed him and appealing to the romantic persuasions of the hotel management, three weeks later they were married in the very spot he'd first laid eyes on her.

For all the unpredictability of their courtship, the wedding ceremony was a storybook affair. There was not a dry eye in the place as Cassie walked down the aisle on her father's arm to join Charlie at the altar. It wasn't just that they looked picture perfect, she in her elegant white Valencia beaded dress with a full train and he in his formal gray morning suit. It was the confident expression on the bride's face, the tender pride in the lively gray eyes of the groom's.

At the altar, side by side and hand in hand, they exchanged speaking looks. Drawing in a deep breath, Cassie arched a brow at him, as if to say, how did we get here? Smiling confidently, he squeezed her hand in return. She couldn't quite believe this moment was finally happening. It was like a dream, like it was happening to somebody else.

And then Cassie happened to glance at Charlie's shoes, looked again. Beside her, at her right, Fran, her matron of honor, saw the glance and stared down, as well. And then Joe, the best man, caught on, and finally even the minister glanced up from his Bible to stare at Charlie's shoes. At the unexpected interruption in the ceremony, a nervous twitter went up from the crowd.

Cassie's eyes shot to her husband-to-be's. "Charlie Whitman," she whispered. "Are you wearing Reeboks?"

Aware of the four pairs of eyes upon him, he defended his choice. "Hey, they're black, aren't they? And they're new." He'd bought them specially, wanting something of himself in this ceremony.

Cassie and Fran exchanged looks. Charlie Whitman was as outrageous as ever.

Charlie's eyes softened. "Cassie, I'm sor—"

With a little laugh, Cassie interrupted him. "I like them. For a minute there you looked so glamorous I thought I was marrying the wrong guy."

But he was the right guy, the one and only guy for her. Not many men would wear sneakers to their wedding, and not many women would be touched by it.

Charlie's incongruous footwear seemed to set the tone for the lively reception that followed. Their guests, despite all their finery, acted in character. Mr. Gorham flirted with a blonde from catering while Mrs. Gorham pretended not to notice. Cassie's mother and father wandered around snapping pictures of everything for their scrapbook and declaring it all too swank for words. Her nieces and nephews whooped around the place, laughing and running, much to the consternation of the hotel staff. Fran insisted that this had all been her doing, while Joe silently beamed. And Mr. and Mrs. Whitman III argued incessantly about which one of them deserved credit for the smashing success Charlie had made of his life. At least, Sylvia argued while Charlie's father barked, "What?"

Charlie had debated about whether to invite them, then decided to let bygones be bygones. As he'd told Cassie, "Hey, they can't hurt me anymore, right?" In the face of his new maturity, Cassie could only agree.

As for the bride and groom, they sat speechless at the head table, wearing the stunned, dazed looks of two people surrounded by the combined forces of everyone they loved most in the world.

"Whose idea was it anyway, this circus, Armstrong?" Charlie felt compelled to ask.

"Yours," she shot back. "And the name is Whitman, Whitman. And don't you ever forget it."

Bringing her hand to his lips, he grazed her knuckles with a kiss. "Never," he told her, smiling into her eyes. "Till death do us part." A trace of the old insecurity flared. "Believe me?"

Cassie's expression grew soft and luminous. "Always. I'll always believe in you. I always have and I always will."

"You always were a soft touch," he teased, making her laugh even as he tilted her face for a kiss.

THEY WERE STILL LAUGHING seven months later when he was cradling his wife while she held their sleeping son. The hospital bed seemed like home with the three of them in it. Like any new parents, Charlie and Cassie stared into that tiny, scrunched-up face, examined those teeny, tiny fingers and marveled at the life they had created together. Already, they thought the baby looked like them with his thatch of curly dark hair and blue, blue eyes. The nursery staff didn't have the heart to tell them that all newborns looked like that. "It's a miracle, isn't it, Charlie?" Cassie breathed.

It certainly was. Charlie couldn't even begin to find the words for all he was feeling, and he didn't even try. "So, what are we going to name this kid? We can't keep on calling him Baby forever. Personally, I think he looks like a tough guy. You know, like a Bubba type, especially if he inherits his mother's right hook."

Smiling, Cassie looked up from the six-pound bundle. "Not Charles the Fifth, I take it?"

Charlie shook his head. "Never. Anything but that. We are not carrying on the Whitman family tradition." He reached out a finger to the bundle, his eyes brimming with unexpected tears when the small fist curled tightly about his own. The baby's grip was surprisingly strong, surprisingly powerful, as if he already knew he belonged to this man. "No," Charlie said. "This is one child who's always going to know he's loved."

Cassie heard the note in his voice. Her eyes turned to her husband. "I think he already does."

IT WAS LITTLE Christopher Armstrong Whitman who came home from the hospital with his mommy and daddy to the brand-new nursery awaiting him. By mutual consent, Charlie and Cassie had given up their city apartments and chosen a stately colonial in the suburbs of Westchester County. Charlie had checked out the school district, a move Cassie found hysterically funny and very touching. But then, Charlie Whitman had never done anything by half measure in his life, and fatherhood proved no exception.

"I don't know, Charlie," Cassie said as they flopped into bed one night, exhausted from a full day of caring for an infant. "For a guy who doesn't like commitments very much, you've sure gotten yourself into a heck of a mess."

Fast-of-foot, fleet-of-mouth, Charlie I'll-Try-Anything-for-a-Year Whitman was now Charlie Whitman, family man. He had an infant son, a mortgage, and, since they'd both agreed Cassie would go to school part-time to raise their child, an unemployed wife and an advance on his second novel, the deadline looming. He'd sold the first, and everyone thought he had a bright future in front of him. Charlie had to agree, although it wasn't his writing career he was thinking of. These days, Charlie Whitman wouldn't have traded places with anyone in the world. After a lifetime of searching and one of the longest adolescences in history, Charlie Whitman had finally come home.

It was Cassie who grew wistful for a moment, remembering the night they'd met and the two people they used to be, those halcyon days before diapers and bottles and midnight feedings. In particular, she recalled a tall, lanky stranger with curly hair and lively gray eyes, a man who had bribed a hotel employee, lied about holding a union card and then practically seduced her on the dance floor. About to shut off the bedside light, she paused, then impulsively extended her hand to her husband. "Well, Charlie Whitman, to a rewarding and productive next fifty years."

He remembered that long-ago evening, too. He favored her with a mock salute and an even bigger grin. "Let the games begin, Cassie Armstrong Whitman."

And as their lips and their laughter mingled, they knew that whatever life threw their way, they'd always be together and they'd always have fun.

BRIDE'S BAY RESORT

UNLOCK THE DOOR TO GREAT ROMANCE AT BRIDE'S BAY RESORT

Join Harlequin's new across-the-lines series, set in an exclusive hotel on an island off the coast of South Carolina.

Seven of your favorite authors will bring you exciting stories about fascinating heroes and heroines discovering love at Bride's Bay Resort.

Look for these fabulous stories coming to a store near you beginning in January 1996.

Harlequin American Romance #613 in January
Matchmaking Baby by Cathy Gillen Thacker

Harlequin Presents #1794 in February
Indiscretions by Robyn Donald

Harlequin Intrigue #362 in March
Love and Lies by Dawn Stewardson

Harlequin Romance #3404 in April
Make Believe Engagement by Day Leclaire

Harlequin Temptation #588 in May
Stranger in the Night by Roseanne Williams

Harlequin Superromance #695 in June
Married to a Stranger by Connie Bennett

Harlequin Historicals #324 in July
Dulcie's Gift by Ruth Langan

Visit Bride's Bay Resort each month wherever
Harlequin books are sold.

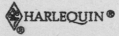

HARLEQUIN ®

MILLION DOLLAR SWEEPSTAKES
AND
EXTRA BONUS PRIZE DRAWING

No purchase necessary. To enter the sweepstakes, follow the directions published and complete and mail your Official Entry Form. If your Official Entry Form is missing, or you wish to obtain an additional one (limit: one Official Entry Form per request, one request per outer mailing envelope) send a separate, stamped, self-addressed #10 envelope (4 1/8" X 9 1/2") via first-class mail to: Million Dollar Sweepstakes and Extra Bonus Prize Drawing Entry Form, P.O. Box 1867, Buffalo, NY 14269-1867. Request must be received no later than January 15, 1998. For eligibility into the sweepstakes, entries must be received no later than March 31,1998. No liability is assumed for printing errors, lost, late, non-delivered or misdirected entries. Odds of winning are determined by the number of eligible entries distributed and received.

Sweepstakes open to residents of the U.S. (except Puerto Rico), Canada and Europe who are 18 years of age or older. All applicable laws and regulations apply. Sweepstakes offer void wherever prohibited by law. Values of all prizes are in U.S. currency. This sweepstakes is presented by Torstar Corp., its subsidiaries and affiliates, in conjunction with book, merchandise and/or product offerings. For a copy of the Official Rules governing this sweepstakes, send a self-addressed, stamped envelope (WA residents need not affix return postage) to: MILLION DOLLAR SWEEP-STAKES AND EXTRA BONUS PRIZE DRAWING Rules, P.O. Box 4470, Blair, NE 68009-4470, USA.

FAST CASH 4033 DRAW RULES
NO PURCHASE OR OBLIGATION NECESSARY

Fifty prizes of $50 each will be awarded in random drawings to be conducted no later than 6/28/96 from amongst all eligible responses to this prize offer received as of 5/14/96. To enter, follow directions, affix 1st-class postage and mail OR write Fast Cash 4033 on a 3" x 5" card along with your name and address and mail that card to: Harlequin's Fast Cash 4033 Draw, P.O. Box 1395, Buffalo, NY 14240-1395 OR P.O. Box 618, Fort Erie, Ontario L2A 5X3. (Limit: one entry per outer envelope; all entries must be sent via 1st-class mail.) Limit: one prize per household. Odds of winning are determined by the number of eligible responses received. Offer is open only to residents of the U.S. (except Puerto Rico) and Canada and is void wherever prohibited by law. All applicable laws and regulations apply. Any litigation within the province of Quebec respecting the conduct and awarding of a prize in this sweepstakes may be submitted to the Régie des alcools, des courses et des jeux. In order for a Canadian resident to win a prize, that person will be required to correctly answer a time-limited arithmetical skill-testing question to be administered by mail. Names of winners available after 7/30/96 by sending a self-addressed, stamped envelope to: Fast Cash 4033 Draw Winners, P.O. Box 4200, Blair, NE 68009-4200.

SWP-H3ZD

#582 NOBODY'S HERO
by Patricia Keelyn

Meet Sam Cooper, P.I. He's cynical and jaded. A real loner. This rogue only takes cases that he can't get involved in emotionally. But then gorgeous Jessie Burkett comes to him for help. And he realizes he'd like to become involved with her, intimately....

All men are not created equal. Some are rough around the edges. Tough-minded but tenderhearted. Incredibly sexy. The tempting fulfillment of every woman's fantasy.

When it's time to fight for what they believe in, to win that special woman, our Rebels and Rogues are heroes at heart.

Look for NOBODY'S HERO in April 1996, wherever Harlequin books are sold.

HARLEQUIN SUPERROMANCE®

From the bestselling author of
THE TAGGARTS OF TEXAS!
comes

Cupid, Colorado...

This is ranch country, cowboy country—a land of high mountains
and swift, cold rivers, of deer, elk and bear. The land is important
here—family and neighbors are, too. 'Course, you have the chance
to really get to know your neighbors in Cupid. Take the Camerons,
for instance. The first Cameron came to Cupid more than a hundred
years ago, and Camerons have owned and worked the Straight Arrow
Ranch—the largest spread in these parts—ever since.

For kids and kisses, tears and laughter, wild horses and wilder men—
come to the Straight Arrow Ranch, near Cupid, Colorado. Come meet
the Camerons.

THE CAMERONS OF COLORADO
by Ruth Jean Dale

Kids, Critters and Cupid (Superromance #678)
available in February 1996

The Cupid Conspiracy (Temptation #579)
available in March 1996

The Cupid Chronicles (Superromance #687)
available in April 1996

Harlequin invites you to the
wedding of the century!

This April be prepared to catch the bouquet with
the glamorous debut of

Weddings by DeWilde

For years, DeWildes—the elegant and fashionable
wedding store chain—has helped brides around the
world turn the fantasy of their special day into reality.
But now the store and three generations of family are
torn apart by divorce. As family members face new
challenges and loves, a long-secret mystery begins to
unravel.... Set against an international backdrop of
London, Paris, New York and Sydney, this new series
features the glitzy, fast-paced world of designer wedding
fashions and missing heirlooms!

In April watch for:
SHATTERED VOWS
by Jasmine Cresswell

Look in the back pages of *Weddings by DeWilde* for
details about our fabulous sweepstakes contest to win a
real diamond ring!

Coming this April to your favorite retail outlet.

WBDT

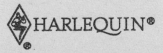
HARLEQUIN®

Fall in love all over again with

This Time... MARRIAGE

In this collection of original short stories, three brides get a unique chance for a return engagement!

- Being kidnapped from your bridal shower by a one-time love can really put a crimp in your wedding plans! *The Borrowed Bride*— by **Susan Wiggs**, *Romantic Times* Career Achievement Award-winning author.

- After fifteen years a couple reunites for the sake of their child—this time will it end in marriage? *The Forgotten Bride*—by **Janice Kaiser**.

- It's tough to make a good divorce stick—especially when you're thrown together with your ex in a magazine wedding shoot! *The Bygone Bride*— by **Muriel Jensen**.

Don't miss THIS TIME...MARRIAGE, available in April wherever Harlequin books are sold.

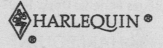

HARLEQUIN ®

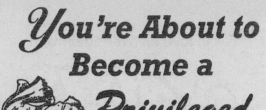

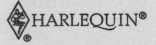